'**Why not come straight out with it and say you can't stand the sight of me?**'

Heat rushed to her face. 'Because it's not true. I don't hate the sight of you.'

'In that case, if I asked you to dinner one evening on more neutral ground, would you say yes?' he demanded.

'No,' she said bluntly.

'I was asking for a few hours of your company, not your hand in marriage,' he said with sudden sarcasm.

'Good,' she retorted, as she wrenched her hand away. 'Because I wouldn't marry you, Mr Smith, if you were the last man on earth.'

Catherine George was born in Wales, and early on developed a passion for reading which eventually fuelled her compulsion to write. Marriage to an engineer led to nine years in Brazil, but on his later travels the education of her son and daughter kept her in the UK. And instead of constant reading to pass her lonely evenings she began to write the first of her romantic novels. When not writing and reading she loves to cook, listen to opera and browse in antiques shops.

Recent titles by the same author:

HUSBAND FOR REAL
RESTLESS NIGHTS

LEGALLY HIS

BY
CATHERINE GEORGE

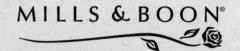

MILLS & BOON®

*MILLS & BOON and MILLS & BOON with the Rose Device
are registered trademarks of the publisher.*

*First published in Great Britain 2001
Harlequin Mills & Boon Limited,
Eton House, 18-24 Paradise Road, Richmond, Surrey TW9 1SR*

© Catherine George 2001

ISBN 0 263 82556 6

*Set in Times Roman 10½ on 12 pt.
01-1201-46233*

*Printed and bound in Spain
by Litografía Rosés, S.A., Barcelona*

PROLOGUE

THE OLD house was austerely beautiful, with architecture straight from the pages of a Jane Austen novel, and the welcome given to visitors unfailingly warm. But the antiquated heating system was a severe drawback to spending a winter night under the house's listed roof. If heat ever managed to rise to the top floor it gave up the struggle long before bedtime, and the current guest lay shivering in the room the son of the house had insisted on turning over to him.

'A bit warmer than the spare,' he was informed cheerfully. 'And mine's a double bed, so you can roll yourself in the quilt if you're cold.'

Not so much cold as deep frozen. But male pride had ruled out a request for a hot-water bottle after the Judge's generous nightcaps of single malt. The visitor lay as still as he could to conserve body heat, and eventually the effects of the whisky and the long car journey took effect.

He woke abruptly to moonlight streaming through the multi-paned window. And blissful warmth. Someone had given him a couple of hot-water bottles after all. He stretched comfortably, then stiffened in horror, every hair erect on the back of his neck. He was sandwiched between two little girls! He swallowed convulsively, heart pounding, his knee-jerk reaction to evict his uninvited guests at the double. But a basic instinct of self-preservation warned that they would scream their heads off if he did, and bring the whole household running.

And this was the household of a judge not famous for
leniency. The guest clamped down hard on chattering
teeth. One of his uninvited bedmates was the eight-year-
old daughter of the house, but the other child was unknown to him. And, if his desperate prayers were
answered, would remain that way. He wasn't given to
praying much. But in his present situation surely
Someone would listen. And be a hell of a sight more
lenient than the Judge if he discovered his son's nine-
teen-year-old friend in bed with two small girls. One of
whom was the apple of her father's eye.

His gorge rose at the thought, the whisky threatening
to follow suit. But with iron will he controlled his di-
gestive system, schooling himself to lie motionless as an
effigy between the sleeping children. And after what
seemed like endless hours of misery, nature eventually
delivered him from his nightmare into the blessed release
of sleep. When he woke for the second time it was broad
daylight. And he was wonderfully, thankfully, alone.

CHAPTER ONE

IT WAS late on a wet, dark Sunday night when Sophie Marlow, in a black, angry mood in keeping with the elements, drove back from London to Gloucestershire. Her mood deteriorated even further when headlights which appeared in her rearview mirror on the turnoff from the motorway stayed with her all the way to Long Ashley, making her very edgy by the time the familiar boundary walls finally came into view through the rain sheeting down in the beam of her headlights.

Five entrances punctuated the walls, each with a small lodge house, four of which were owned by the estate. One of the these was Sophie's home, part of the perks of her job as estate administrator and PA to the director and general manager of Highfield Hall International, the exclusive-use conference centre which had employed her for the past four years. She counted the lodges off as she drove along the narrow, curving road, and blew out her cheeks in relief when the pursuing headlights suddenly vanished from her rearview mirror. The car had turned in at the only privately owned cottage, Ewen and Rosanna Fraser's place. Odd they hadn't let her know they were coming. She turned in at her own gateway at last, relaxing when security lights switched on outside the cottage.

Sophie made a dash through the downpour to unlock the front door and switched on the light in the narrow hall, her spirits rising further at the welcome sight of her own apricot walls and white painted plasterwork. Glen

Taylor, until recently the male presence in her life, had urged her to paint the beautiful covings and dados black against grey walls—worse still, to exchange her chintz and watercolours for black leather and Japanese prints in minimalist style totally alien to a Victorian cottage. After today's disaster Sophie could only thank her lucky stars she'd firmly refused to let him move in with her, as he'd wanted.

With a shudder at the very idea, she dumped her bags down and went to the kitchen to listen to her messages while the kettle boiled.

'Hi, Sophie,' said Stephen Laing, her boss. 'Ewen Fraser rang to say he's letting a friend stay at his cottage for a while to finish a book. Name of Smith. I promised Ewen you'd look after his pal well, so make time to pay a call on him to confirm his requirements as to catering, cleaning, etc. See you Tuesday.'

Hoping he meant Murray Smith, one of her favourite authors, Sophie listened to her second message.

'Hi, Sophie. Luce here. Ring me for a chat.'

'*Sophie*!' said the last voice, which was male, familiar and furious. 'What the hell did you take off like that for? Ring me. *Now*.'

Not now. Not ever. Sophie glared balefully at the machine, made a note to visit Ewen Fraser's tenant, but postponed the call to her friend until next day. She made herself a cup of tea and curled up on the sofa in her small sitting room, feeling as though she'd survived some life-threatening disaster. Glen Taylor, until recently head chef at Highfield Hall, was a genius in the kitchen, with the volatile temperament that went with the territory. But today he'd overstepped the mark so far Sophie never wanted to lay eyes on him again. Deep down, even in the beginning, when he'd been at his most charming and persuasive, she'd always veered away from something unsettling about Glen; the indefinable something he brought to the genius which had quickly made the Highfield restaurant so renowned. Stephen Laing had been furious when Glen threw up his job after only a few months to open a place of his own in London.

'He'll find that working for himself is a different ball-game, TV chef or not,' Stephen told Sophie. 'Glen may have been cock of the walk here at Highfield, but in London he'll be a very small fish in a huge, competitive pond. So if you're wise you'll steer well clear of his business affairs.'

Sophie had great respect for Stephen Laing's acumen. And common sense of her own. So today, when Glen had taken it for granted she would not only sink her savings into his new venture but also give up her job and her home and work as his manager for free until the business got going, she'd laughed in his face and refused. At first, Glen hadn't believed her, so sure of her consent he'd thought she was teasing, and tried to bring her round with sexual persuasion which turned ugly when she remained obdurate.

'You'll come running back,' he'd sneered, when Sophie stormed out of his flat. 'You're mad about me, and you know it.'

Mad to have had anything to do with him, thought Sophie, seething. Glen's looks were a great success on television cooking programmes. And in the beginning she had liked him well enough. But today whatever luke-warm feelings she'd had left for him had vanished entirely. Her mouth twisted in angry distaste. She could see Glen Taylor all too clearly now that their short relationship was over. He'd made it plain from the beginning that he wanted her in his bed. But it was obvious in hindsight that he'd felt equal lust—possibly more—for her administrative skills.

To damp down the temper still boiling away inside her Sophie went off to lie chin-deep in steaming bubbles, only to groan in frustration when the doorbell rang the moment she'd begun to relax. She jumped out of the bath, tied on a towelling robe, twisted a towel into a turban round her wet hair, and ran downstairs. Then came skidding to a halt in the hall, suddenly afraid that Glen might have come chasing down from London after her.

Afraid? Sophie squared her shoulders, opened the door a crack as far as the safety chain allowed, and peered up into eyes which were the only feature visible between the brim of a dripping hat and the upturned collar of a caped raincoat.

'Good evening,' said the stranger. 'Miss Marlow?'

'Yes?'

'Sorry to disturb you. My name's Jago Smith. I'm staying at the Frasers' place for a while.'

Not Murray Smith, then. Pity. Sophie smiled politely. 'How do you do? Is there something you need?'

The man shook his head, spraying raindrops so liberally he dodged back quickly into the shadows. 'No thanks—at least not right now. But Ewen advised introducing myself right away, to show I'm not squatting illegally.'

'I already knew about you, Mr Smith,' she assured him. 'A message was waiting for me when I got home just now.'

The eyes dropped to her bare feet. 'I should have rung instead of barging in like this. My apologies.'

'Not at all. Did Ewen mention that I'm the estate administrator? I can arrange for anything you need.'

'Thank you. Perhaps we could discuss that tomorrow? At a time convenient to you, of course.'

Odd, thought Sophie. All she could see was a pair of eyes, but something about the stranger appealed to her. Strongly. 'I usually finish about six-thirty,' she said, after a pause. 'Perhaps you'd call round then.'

'Better still, I could give you a drink at Ewen's place.'

Sophie thought it over for a moment, then nodded. 'Right. About seven, then.'

He touched a finger to his hatbrim, said goodnight and sprinted down the path through the downpour. Sophie closed her front door, refastened the chain, and for the first time since she'd lived at Ivy Lodge slammed the substantial bolt into place. Glen's fault. Today he'd succeeded in making her physically afraid for the first time in her life. Cursing herself for letting him have a key, she added a change of locks to her check-list for next day. Just in case.

First thing next morning Sophie told the startled receptionist that she was permanently unavailable to Glen Taylor if he should ring. Then as usual she began her day by changing the closed circuit television tape before sorting the mail, and afterwards made a start on the dictation tape Stephen had left for her. While she worked she dealt with a constant stream of phone calls, one of which, as was often the case, was a routine request to land a helicopter. She confirmed that the helipad and surrounding area would be free at the requested time, sent a memo to all heads of department to inform them when the helicopter would be landing, then gave lunch in the staff restaurant a miss to hurry home through the rain to meet the locksmith.

Afterwards, feeling much happier with a new set of keys in her possession, Sophie went back to the Hall to collect her messages from Reception. In her office she discarded two from Glen, unread, and settled down to return the others. Due to constant interruptions from the phone it took her the rest of the afternoon to complete the minutes of a meeting she'd taken the previous Friday, but at last she was able to take advantage of Stephen's absence to leave on time for once. Grateful, as always, for not having to commute, she walked home through an evening no longer full of rain, but dark enough to keep her to the main, floodlit walkways.

When Sophie arrived home there were more furious messages from Glen, who was savage with rage after being ignored all day. The theme of all three messages was the same. He would forgive her if she did what he wanted. Otherwise she would be sorry.

Sophie was already sorry. Sorry she'd ever met him.

She rang Lucy to give her the news, by this time able to laugh when her friend described Glen Taylor in words so graphic that Sophie's ears burned.

'You're well shot of him,' said her friend forcefully. 'I could never understand what you saw in him. I know he's a genius with a frying pan, and all that, but I can only suppose he's even more inspired in bed.'

'*Frying pan!* Glen would blow a fuse if he heard that one.'

'I was always afraid he would, you know.'

'He almost did yesterday. But don't worry, he won't get the chance again.'

After Lucy rang off Sophie raced through a shower and dried her hair at top speed. Afterwards, dressed in black trousers and a sweater the same russet shade of her hair, she made sure all her new locks were secured, belted on a long black trenchcoat, collected umbrella and torch and set off for the cottage Ewen Fraser had inherited from his great uncle.

The door opened the moment she rang the bell, to reveal Jago Smith under the hall light, smiling in welcome. Sophie's answering smile was warm for a split second. Then it died abruptly. Her heart gave a sickening lurch as recognition stabbed her like a knife. Without the raincoat and hat of the night before Jago Smith was revealed as tall and slim-hipped in a vivid green wool shirt and outrageously tight jeans, his dark waving hair a frame for a good-looking, confident face she remembered only too well.

'Good evening, Miss Marlow. Come in.' Unaware of the shell-shock his visitor was suffering, he ushered her into a sitting room identical to her own in size and shape, with comfortable sofas, shelves full of blue and white porcelain, walls literally covered with pictures, and on a small table a tray with glasses and a bottle of wine flanked by a crystal dish of nuts. 'Let me take your coat and give you a drink.'

Sophie pulled herself together. 'No thanks,' she said shortly. 'I can't stay. If you'll just tell me what you need, I must get back.'

His grey eyes narrowed. 'In which case, rather than waste your time, Miss Marlow, I could have phoned and saved you the walk over here tonight.'

A better idea all round if only she'd recognised him the night before. Sophie took a notebook from her bag and got down to business. 'But since I am here, Mr Smith, I'll jot down a few details. I can arrange cleaning, laundry, even catering if you want. The restaurant at the Hall is excellent, but if you prefer to eat here they'll send food over.'

'So Ewen told me,' he said, his eyes trained on her

face. 'The cottage is still reasonably tidy for the time being, mainly because I'm working upstairs in the Frasers' spare bedroom. But a quick blitz from someone now and then would be good. But only for an hour or two. I can't concentrate with someone in the house.'

'I'll arrange for one of the cleaners to come and chat with you,' said Sophie, avoiding eye contact. 'You can work out what you want, laundry included, even food-shopping if you want.'

He shook his head. 'I'll organise that for myself via the Internet. I'll rustle up a meal for myself most evenings, but it's good to know I can order in if I'm lazy. Is that what you do?' he added.

'Only on special occasions. Normally I cook for myself.' And in the past sometimes for Glen, who'd refused to practise his skills in her kitchen. Sophie wanted badly to go, but, mindful of Stephen Laing's instructions to do her best for Ewen's guest, she couldn't quite bring herself to turn tail and run. 'Are you writing a novel?' she asked politely.

He shook his head. 'Non-fiction. A collection of legal trials. I'm a lawyer by profession, but I take a break occasionally to write.' His eyes narrowed as they picked up on her reaction. 'Something tells me you don't care for lawyers.'

'Why do you say that?'

'Perhaps you agree with Shakespeare on the subject.'

Sophie thought hard for a moment. 'Oh. Right. ''First let's kill all the lawyers''?' Some of them, anyway. 'I did it in school, but I can't remember where it comes from.'

'*Henry VI*, part two,' he said so promptly Sophie smiled faintly.

'The subject's obviously come up before.'

'Only with the more erudite of my acquaintance.'

She put the notebook back in her bag. 'Right. I must go. If you think of anything else, Mr Smith, just ring me.'

'Thank you. I may have to take you up on that,' he said, as he saw her into the hall. 'My flight to the country was unexpected. I became suddenly homeless recently, and Ewen Fraser came to my rescue while I sort out somewhere else to live.'

Sophie couldn't help wondering why he'd needed rescuing. Abrupt end of an affair, perhaps, even a marriage. Though a good-looking, successful barrister who wrote in his spare time would hardly be left lamenting long.

Sophie took out a card and handed it to him. 'My phone numbers, office and home. And now I'll leave you to get on with your book. Goodnight, Mr Smith.'

'I'll walk back with you.'

Sophie's chin lifted. 'There's absolutely no need—'

He looked down his nose at her. 'It's dark, and it's down to me that you're here in the first place. I'll see you home.'

Cursing his good manners, she waited impatiently while he shrugged into the caped raincoat of the night before and locked the door. Keeping her distance, Sophie shone her torch as they made their way across the parkland to Ivy Lodge, wishing that her high-heeled boots were running shoes so she could move faster over the grass, because for the life of her she couldn't break the silence which hung over them like a thundercloud. As they came in sight of Ivy Lodge the silence was shattered by the sound of breaking glass, and ignoring her high heels Sophie took off for home like an Olympic sprinter, with Jago in close pursuit. At the cottage gate he thrust her behind him as the security lights revealed a man using a scarf to staunch the blood welling from a cut on his hand.

'Glen!' exclaimed Sophie in disgust. 'What on *earth* are you doing?'

'Bleeding to death for all you care.' He glared at her. 'You've changed the bloody locks!'

'What if I have? It doesn't give you the right to break my sitting room window,' she retorted furiously. 'Go away. Now. In case you didn't get the message yesterday you're not welcome here any more.'

'You little—' He lunged for her, but a long, relentless hand thrust flat against his chest, holding him off.

'I think not,' drawled a cold voice.

'And just who the hell are you?' howled Glen, incensed.

'Miss Marlow's lawyer. And you, Mr—'

'Taylor,' said Sophie.

'You, Mr Taylor,' Jago went on, 'have some explaining to do.' He turned to Sophie. 'Miss Marlow, call the police.'

It took some time for Sophie to persuade Jago that the police were unnecessary. But he made a point of standing over Glen in her kitchen later, while Sophie saw to the unremarkable surface cut. She doused it with antiseptic and bound on a dressing with chef's blue sticking plaster, the entire process conducted in stony silence Glen was obviously bursting to break.

'Right,' he snapped, when she'd finished, and jerked his head at the man watching the proceedings. 'Outside, please. I want a word with Sophie in private.'

Jago eyed him with grim disapproval. 'I strongly advise my client against this.'

'You can say what you want in front of Mr Smith,' Sophie said briskly.

Glen's eyes flashed ominously. 'But it's *personal*!'

'Mr Smith won't mind.'

'Well *I* do. This is bloody ridiculous—'

'Not as far as I'm concerned,' said Sophie flatly. 'I have no intention of seeing you alone again, Glen. Ever. So say what you have to say and go.'

He stared at her in outrage. 'You actually expect me to drive back to London again tonight with an injured hand?'

'You bet I do. Or you can beg a room up at the Hall, because you're certainly not staying here.'

Glen's face crimsoned with anger. 'Are you serious?'

'Deadly serious!'

'What else must Miss Marlow say, or do, to convince you?' enquired Jago coldly, and turned to Sophie. 'I can slap an injunction on Mr Taylor if you wish.'

She pretended to think about it. 'I think not. At least not for the present.'

Glen stared at her, flabbergasted. 'Sophie, what the hell has got into you? You know how much I care for you.'

'Oh *please*, spare me the pathos!' She speared him with a scornful look. 'Besides, if you do care, you've got a strange way of showing it.'

He threw out his hands in appeal. 'Yesterday was just a one-off, darling, I swear. It won't happen again.'

Sophie nodded emphatically. 'You're right. It won't.'

'Do I take it that Mr Taylor offered you physical violence when you refused to comply with his wishes?' asked her newly acquired lawyer.

'It's none of your damn business—' began Glen hotly, but Jago held up a hand.

'As Miss Marlow's lawyer it most certainly is my business.' He raised a questioning eyebrow at Sophie.

'I don't wish to discuss it further,' she said firmly. 'It's over and done with. Except for the broken window. And I'll send you the bill for that, Glen.'

Speechless, he glared from one to the other for a moment. 'You'll be sorry for this, Sophie,' he said, his voice unsteady with rage.

'Is that a threat, Mr Taylor?' pounced Jago.

Glen, very obviously wanting to let fly with his fists, controlled himself with effort as he turned to Sophie. 'How the hell did you manage to get yourself a lawyer so quickly?'

'Through mutual friends,' said the self-appointed advocate smoothly, and without touching Glen in any way manoevred him out through the front door.

'Goodbye, Glen,' said Sophie with relief.

'You haven't heard the last of this,' he hissed, then cast a fulminating glance at Jago. 'All right, all right, I'm going.' He stared at Sophie irresolutely for a moment, then flung away, stormed down the path to his car and took off through the entrance gate with an ear-splitting scream of tyres.

CHAPTER TWO

SOPHIE watched him out of sight, then looked up at Jago in apology. 'Sorry to involve you in that.'

'You look shaken,' said Jago. 'Make yourself some coffee while I do something about your window.'

'Oh, Lord, I'd forgotten that,' she said wearily, and closed the front door with a bang, cursing the fates for making her beholden to this man, of all men.

Shortly afterwards the cracked pane of glass was re-inforced with layers of polythene cut from refuse sacks and secured with masking tape. And Sophie had made a pot of coffee she felt obliged to share with her guest.

'You look better,' said Jago.

'I feel better.' She breathed in deeply. 'That was all very unpleasant. Embarrassing, too.'

He took the beaker she offered him. 'Was Taylor your fiancé? I'm asking from a purely professional point of view,' he added quickly. 'If it comes to an injunction I'd need to know if he was living here.'

'No.' Sophie felt a sudden unaccountable need to explain. 'I haven't known him long. He was the head chef here until recently, and we occasionally went out together. He persuaded me to let him have a key so he could relax here in the day sometimes when he had time off while I was working.' Her chin lifted. 'But he very definitely didn't live here.'

'But he wanted to, I take it?'

She nodded reluctantly.

'He's no longer here at Highfield?' asked Jago.

'No. Glen started appearing on TV a bit recently, and on the strength of it decided to open a restaurant of his own in London. He wanted me to go with him.'

'You didn't care for the idea?'

'Certainly not. It was never that kind of relationship.' Sophie's eyes flashed coldly. 'And my company was by no means the main attraction. He expected me to throw everything up here to work as his manager until the restaurant takes off. If it ever does.'

Jago frowned. 'You refused, of course?'

'You bet I did.' Her eyes kindled. 'In the end I drove to London to tell him that face to face, because he just wouldn't take no for an answer over the phone. Big mistake.'

Jago smiled crookedly. 'I'm sorry you had all this hassle tonight, but oddly enough I'm grateful to your Mr Taylor.'

Sophie frowned. 'Grateful?'

'For your thaw towards me, slight though it is. Last night I got you out of the bath, yet you were friendly. Tonight, having gone of your own free will to see me, you were the ice queen personified. Will you tell me why?'

Not a chance. 'If I was rude I apologise,' she said stiffly. 'But thanks for your help. Both with my intruder and my window.'

There was silence while his eyes held hers. 'I know this sounds like the corniest line in the book,' he said at last, 'but I can't help feeling we've met before.'

She shook her head. 'No. We haven't.'

He looked unconvinced. 'Perhaps it was in a former life,' he said at last, and drank the last of his coffee. 'Time I left you in peace. You look exhausted.'

She nodded wryly. 'I feel exhausted.'

'Emotional strain. How long have you lived here?'

'I moved in a few months after I came here, four years ago. Are you staying long?' she added casually.

'Ewen's letting me have his place for a month. If I haven't finished the book by that time I must get back to work anyway, or incur the wrath of my head of chambers, not to mention the head clerk. Thank you for the coffee,' he added.

'Thank you again for your help,' she returned formally as she saw him to the door.

He shrugged. 'You'd probably have coped perfectly well without me.'

'The mood Glen was in when we arrived I have my doubts about that!'

'If you have any trouble with him in future let me know.'

'Even if I do, somehow I think I'll only have to mention ''my lawyer'' to put an end to it.' Sophie gave him a wry little smile. '''My lawyer'', indeed!'

'I'm very happy to serve you in that capacity,' he assured her. 'Or in any other. Goodnight. Sleep well.'

Far from sleeping well, Sophie tossed and turned far into the night, cursing fate for bringing her into contact with Jago Smith, who was a man she could have liked a lot. If he were anyone else. But he wasn't. So she would just ignore the fact that fate had sent him to live virtually on her doorstep for a while and, after he'd gone, forget she'd ever encountered him again.

Sophie woke next morning feeling that with Glen Taylor gone from her life a great burden should have been lifted from her shoulders. Instead she'd acquired one of a different kind in the shape of Jago Smith, as he seemed to want to be known. Maybe it was his pen name. She forced her mind away from him while she ate breakfast, then rang a glazier, arranged to meet him at the cottage during her lunch hour, and afterwards, in a tailored black suit, her vivid hair twisted up into its usual, working-day coil, she walked across the park to Highfield Hall to find Stephen Laing already in his office. Sophie made coffee to share with him while she brought him up to speed on everything at Highfield since she'd seen him last, including the official break-up with Glen Taylor.

'Thank God for that,' said Stephen with profound relief. He was a slim man in his early forties, with a thin, intelligent face, and he was, Sophie knew, fond of her. The feeling was mutual, their working relationship harmonious, and before Glen Taylor's arrival on the scene Anna Laing had often invited Sophie to Sunday lunch, or to one of the parties she gave at frequent intervals.

'Perhaps we'll see a bit more of you now,' Stephen said with satisfaction, and eyed her searchingly. 'I hope it didn't end in tears, Sophie.'

'Not mine,' she assured him, and smiled. 'More likely Glen's when I turned down the alluring post of unpaid dogsbody in his new restaurant.'

'That must have gone down well!'

Sophie confirmed that it hadn't, and gave a colourful account of the window-breaking incident the night before, including the part where Jago Smith introduced himself as her lawyer.

Stephen laughed his head off. 'I'd like to have been a fly on the wall!' He eyed her curiously. 'What's this Smith chap like, by the way? I haven't met him myself.'

'He's a lawyer,' said Sophie, her tone so flat Stephen chuckled. 'I'd better get on,' she said briskly. 'I need to get home on the dot at lunchtime. Hot date with a glazier!'

*   *   *

After the drama of the night before, happy in the knowledge that her window was secure, Sophie was glad of a peaceful evening with a book. Glen had actually been gone from Highfield for a fortnight. But tonight, for the first time, she felt truly free of his abrasive presence in her life.

When the phone rang she let the message play in case it was Glen, but Jago Smith's clipped, distinctive tones sent her hurrying to pick up the receiver. Out of curiosity.

'I just wondered whether you managed to get your window fixed today,' he asked.

'I have,' she assured him.

'No more problem with the jilted chef?'

'None so far.'

'All right with your world, then?'

'Pretty much. How did you get on with the cleaner I sent over?'

'Like a house on fire. She's coming in the morning to clean for an hour. Quite long enough, the impressive Angela assures me, to see me shipshape. I'm grateful to you.'

'Not at all, it's my job.' She paused. 'Thanks again for your help last night.'

'No thanks necessary. I'm happy to oblige any time. With that particular problem, or any other.'

Sophie stared moodily at her reflection in the hall mirror. 'That's very kind of you.'

'Miss Marlow—Sophie. I can't see how it's possible, since we've only just met, nevertheless I get the distinct impression I've offended you in some way.'

'Of course you haven't.'

'Then is there something about my person you find repellent?' he demanded.

Quite the reverse. 'No, not in the least.'

'I'd be happier if you'd said that with more conviction!' He paused for a moment. 'I was deeply disappointed when you refused to stay for a drink last night.'

'Just as well I didn't in the circumstances—who knows what damage Glen might have done? Thank you for ringing. Goodnight.'

Sophie went upstairs in thoughtful mood. Jago Smith, it was flatteringly obvious, was interested in her. Or maybe his interest was caught because she was distant with him, when other women were probably anything but. A pity she hadn't hidden her first reaction to him better, of course, but the shock of recognition had caught her off guard. So had the bitter blow of discovering how much she could have been attracted to him if he—and she—were different people.

After putting Jago Smith firmly from her mind, the following day passed much as usual for Sophie. The new chef was making his mark in the restaurant, and, she was told with much thanksgiving by one of the sous chefs, giving his underlings a far easier life than the irascible Glen Taylor. Invited by the restaurant manager to dine there that evening, to pass verdict on the new chef's expertise, Sophie accepted with pleasure, and promised to give Stephen a full report next day.

'Anna was very pleased to hear you've given Glen his marching orders, Sophie,' he told her, when she was ready to leave. 'She rang a few minutes ago to ask if you were free for lunch Sunday week.'

Sophie was very happy to accept. Anna's lunches were relaxed affairs, with children and dogs and various relatives and friends making up the numbers, but due to Glen's recent monopoly of her Sundays, she'd seen neither the Laings nor her own family for much too long.

When Sophie got home she rang her mother for her twice-weekly chat, and gave her deeply relieved parent the news about Glen, then got ready to go out again. Because the restaurant catered to the general public as well as conference guests, she always made an extra effort with her appearance on the rare occasions she dined there. In a mood to celebrate her official break-up with Glen, she chose a wool tunic the colour of cayenne pepper to wear with chocolate suede trousers she'd bought in one of her wilder moments, then went downstairs to polish up brown leather boots with the high heels she favoured to compensate for her lack of inches.

After a long, pampering session up to her neck in water scented with the expensive bath oil Lucy had given her for her birthday, Sophie wriggled into the hip-hugging trousers, made up her face to complement the vivid tunic, and went to work on thick damp hair which dried to the colour of autumn leaves. Her mouth twisted in a wry little smile as she studied her reflection. All this effort should have been made for some attentive escort, instead of just a busman's holiday in the Highfield Hall restaurant. Someone like Jago Smith? Her eyes dulled. No chance of that. Tonight or any other night.

The restaurant was packed when Sophie went in with Joanna Trenchard, the restaurant manager.

'Full house tonight,' she commented.

Joanna looked round critically, her searching eyes confirming that everything was running smoothly. 'Half conference guests, half general public. Pray that our new chef is on form.'

'His underlings seem to like him a lot better than Glen,' commented Sophie.

'I hope a calmer temperament doesn't mean mediocrity in the kitchen!'

'Monsieur Louis asked if you can spare a moment, Miss Trenchard,' said the sommelier, when he brought their wine.

Joanna went off to talk to the head waiter in the bar outside, leaving Sophie to study the rest of the diners. The conference guests were all men tonight, glad to relax after a gruelling day, but the other diners were couples. Sophie felt a slight pang as she turned away to look at the floodlit lawns outside. Her relationship with Glen had never been important, nor had he been the first man in her life. But now she was officially on her own again she couldn't help feeling just a tad envious of the women dining there with lovers or husbands, or even other women's husbands, for all she knew. When the wonderful aromas coming from other tables reminded her that it was a long time since lunch Sophie turned round to look for her friend and saw Joanna approaching with Jago Smith.

'Sophie,' Joanna said, smiling happily. 'Mr Smith would like to dine here tonight, but there won't be a table free for ages, so I'm sure you won't mind if he joins us.'

'Good evening, Miss Marlow.' Jago's smile was wry. 'I told Miss Trenchard I could easily wait, or have a meal sent over—'

'Certainly not!' said Joanna, frowning at Sophie. 'We're delighted. Aren't we?'

'Of course,' said Sophie, and smiled sweetly. 'Do sit down, Mr Smith.'

'Enough of this Mr and Miss stuff,' said Joanna, as Jago held her chair for her. 'I'm Joanna, and this is Sophie.'

'Jago,' he said, sitting down.

'Jago,' echoed Joanna, gazing up at him in a fluttery

way so much at odds with her usual hyper-efficient persona Sophie wanted to kick her under the table. 'Unusual.'

'Family name,' he said briefly, and applied himself to the menu. 'I must be holding you up.'

'Not at all,' said Joanna, and instructed the waiter to keep their meal back to coincide with their guest's. 'Do have some wine, Jago,' she urged, and filled his glass.

A moment before, Sophie reminded herself, she'd envied the women dining with attentive male companions. Now she'd acquired one. And Joanna would have preferred not to share him. Looking at Jago objectively Sophie didn't blame her friend in the slightest. In a fine black sweater with a fawn needlecord suit, even to a prejudiced eye, he looked good. Better than good in Joanna's eyes, it was obvious.

The meal ordered, Jago leaned back in his chair, regarding both his companions in turn. 'Right. I've been glued to my computer since breakfast, but I'm sure you've both spent a far more eventful day. Tell me about it.'

Joanna obliged promptly, displaying an enthusiasm for her job that Jago obviously respected

'How about you, Sophie?' he asked later.

'Pretty routine stuff,' she said dismissively.

'Rubbish,' protested Joanna. 'Stephen Laing—he's the director and general manager—would be lost without her. By the way, Sophie,' she added casually, 'how's Glen?'

Shorthand for back off, thought Sophie, amused. 'History as far as I'm concerned, Jo.' She tasted her mushroom ravioli with respect. 'The new chef's good!'

The entire meal was excellent, and normally Sophie would have enjoyed the treat. But with Jago Smith casting her an occasional glance over his brochette of salmon, her appetite retired injured before her sorbet arrived.

The three of them drank coffee in the bar afterwards, and the moment she'd downed hers Sophie stood up. 'It's been lovely, but it's time I was off—no, no, please don't get up,' she begged, as Jago rose to his feet.

'I'll walk back with you,' he said firmly.

'But it's early yet,' exclaimed Joanna in open dismay.

'I start work at the crack of dawn.' He smiled at her. 'Deadline looming ever closer. But thank you for coming to my rescue, Joanna. It's been a delightful evening.'

She looked up at him in appeal. 'Perhaps we could do it again some time.'

'I'll look forward to that,' he assured her.

'There was absolutely no need for this,' hissed Sophie, as she left the building with Jago. 'You could have stayed with Joanna.'

He shook his head. 'If you walk home alone you might be besieged by avenging ex-lovers again.'

Her chin lifted. 'That was a one-off. It won't happen again.'

'If it does, ring me and I'll put my lawyer's hat on and come rushing to the rescue.'

Sophie gave him a fulminating look. 'I don't *need* rescuing.'

He raised an eyebrow. 'Never? No hassle from the men at the conferences here?'

'It's my capacity to deal with that kind of thing that makes me good at my job.'

Jago looked unconvinced. 'A woman with looks like yours must inevitably attract male attention, Sophie.'

'Not in my working clothes,' she assured him. 'Tailored suits, hair scraped back and no-nonsense spectacles.'

'Does the disguise work?' he said with amusement.

'It's no disguise—just a practical way to dress for the job.'

He gave her another all-encompassing look as they passed under one of the lights. 'You attracted a fair amount of attention tonight. One of the men at the next table couldn't take his eyes off you.'

She shrugged indifferently. 'I didn't notice.'

'That was obvious. It was left to me to catch his lustful eye and make it plain *I*'d noticed.'

Sophie quelled a rush of pleasure at the thought. 'You needn't have troubled.'

'No trouble. I'll go in to bat for you any time. I've told you that.'

'Quite unnecessary.'

Jago paused as they reached her gate. 'Do you dine often at the Hall?'

'Hardly ever. This was a spot-check on the new chef, and I shall report to my boss in the morning. By the way,' she added, 'what did *you* think of the meal?'

'First class.' His smile was mocking. 'Though it's possible the company contributed to my pleasure.'

'No, seriously,' she said impatiently. 'Was the food up to London standards?'

'Far better than some places I've patronised,' he assured her, and leaned against the gatepost like a man prepared to linger. 'Not that I eat out all the time. In London it's usually something picked up from the deli on my way home. Unless someone's cooking for me. Which was sometimes the case until recently,' he added.

Sophie fought her curiosity and lost. 'Before you were cast into the snow?'

The wind brushed an unruly lock of hair across his forehead as he looked away. 'The lady in question is a barrister with another firm, and we're both busy people. Lately our spare time together coincided less and less.'

Sophie felt an illogical hostility towards the unknown lady. 'She got tired of the arrangement?'

'It seems so.' Jago smiled sardonically. 'I came home unexpectedly one night and found her in bed with a married colleague of ours.'

'Ouch!'

'Exactly. I removed myself to a hotel at top speed. Shortly afterwards I spent an evening with the Frasers, and Ewen offered me his place to finish my book. In the meantime I've put my brother on the trail of possible flats.'

Sophie eyed him curiously. 'Your colleague—the married one. Was he embarrassed when you arrived?'

Jago let out a crack of laughter. 'Lord, yes. So was I!'

'Isn't he worried you'll tell his wife?'

'He knows I would never do that.' Jago's mouth tightened. 'And Isobel airily expected me to forget about it and carry on the same as before.'

Sophie frowned. 'She isn't in love with this man, then?'

'Not in the least.' He lifted a shoulder. 'They had a few drinks after work, one thing led to another, and I was tactless enough to win my case quickly and arrive home a day early. Otherwise I would have known nothing about it. Which made me wonder if it had happened before. When I realised I didn't care if it had I called it a day.' He moved closer. 'But it was no tragedy—in fact, Sophie, on reflection I owe a debt to my philandering colleague.'

'Debt?'

'If he hadn't succumbed to Isobel's considerable charms that night I might never have met you.' Jago winced as Sophie's face closed like a slammed door. 'Hell. Now I've put my foot in it again.'

She looked very deliberately at her watch. 'Time I went in. Thank you for bringing me home.'

'Return to permafrost,' he sighed, and eyed her searchingly, obstructing her way through the gate. 'Tell me why, Sophie Marlow.'

'I'm tired.' She forced a smile. 'Life has been a little hectic lately, one way and another.'

His mouth twisted. 'And I bored you rigid by telling you the story of my life.'

'It was very interesting.' More interesting than Sophie wanted him to know.

'I'd like to hear yours some time.' He moved away from the gate. 'Goodnight, Sophie. Tonight was an unexpected pleasure. Thank you for your company.'

'You had Joanna's company too,' she pointed out.

'True. But it was yours I enjoyed most. And would like to again.' His eyes challenged hers, and Sophie's fell.

'I never mix business with pleasure.' She moved past him, but he caught her hand.

'I'm not one of your conference clients, Sophie. So why not come straight out with it and say you can't stand the sight of me?'

Heat rushed to her face. 'Because it's not true. I don't hate the sight of you.'

'In that case, if I asked you to dinner one evening on more neutral ground, would you say yes?' he demanded.

'No,' she said bluntly. 'At the moment, for reasons

you saw firsthand, I prefer the company of women friends.'

'I was asking for a few hours of your company, not your hand in marriage,' he said with sudden sarcasm.

'Good,' she retorted, as she wrenched her hand away. 'Because I wouldn't marry you, Mr Smith, if you were the last man on earth.'

THE instant the words were out Sophie could have kicked herself. The stony affront on Jago's face haunted her as she made hasty preparations for bed, and she took cover under her quilt, hugging a pillow across her chest for comfort. What a stupid, brainless thing to say, when she'd been so determined to conduct herself with aloof dignity at all times in Jago Smith's company.

As she reached to turn out the light the phone rang.

'Don't put the phone down,' said Jago quickly. 'Are you in bed?'

'Yes,' said Sophie in a constricted voice.

'What was all that about just now?'

She took in a deep breath. 'You were sarcastic. I lost my temper.'

'Is your temper always so volatile?'

'Guilty as charged,' she said flippantly.

'Somehow I doubt that. You obviously meant every word. What in God's name have I done to deserve it?' He waited, but Sophie remained silent. 'You're not going to tell me, are you? Yet I've felt all along that I've met you before,' he went on after a moment. '*Have* we, by any chance, and you resent my lapse of memory?'

'No,' she said woodenly.

He sighed. 'You're a mystery, Sophie Marlow. Perhaps I should cultivate your friend Joanna's acquaintance and see if she can solve it for me.'

Since Joanna was more colleague than close friend,

Jago Smith would have no luck in that direction. 'You can try,' said Sophie.

'Which means I'd have no success. Pity. Goodnight, Sophie.'

'Goodnight.'

Sophie put the receiver down and lay on her back, staring at the ceiling. Jago was so right. It *was* a pity— a great pity—in more ways than he realised.

Next day was hectic. Sophie walked home later than usual through the chilly autumn night, shivering as she kept to the main floodlit paths rather than take the short cut across the park to Ivy Lodge. In the distance she could see lights in the Frasers' cottage, and felt a sharp, unexpected pang of regret. After last night it was unlikely she'd see Jago again. A thought which depressed until she cheered herself up with the prospect of the forthcoming weekend with her family.

With the help of his wife Charlotte her brother Ben ran a large garden centre and nursery in the Vale of Usk, and it was some time since Sophie had seen them, or her mother, who lived in a small flat in a renovated country house nearby. Once she'd arranged the weekend Sophie's longing to see her family grew more intense by the minute, along with her regret for allowing Glen Taylor to monopolise her free time so much she'd neglected her nearest and dearest.

'It's the norm when one's in love,' said Faith Marlow next evening, over supper.

'I was never in *love* with Glen,' said Sophie, making a face.

'Thank God for that. I was watching him yesterday on TV, showing novices how to cook. He made some quite cruel jokes at their expense.' Mrs Marlow chuckled. 'Lovely to know I can criticise. I've been worried.'

Sophie eyed her mother in remorse. 'You needn't have been. It was never the least bit serious on my part.'

'I wish I'd known that. I've been trying hard to think myself into the role of Glen Taylor's future mother-in-law, but it didn't work the way it does with Charlotte.'

'There was never the slightest danger of that,' said Sophie, and scowled. 'Glen wanted a manager for his restaurant, not a wife. And it was my savings which attracted him, not my big brown eyes, Mother dear. He actually expected me to sink money of my own into his venture.'

Her mother stared at her, incensed. 'What a colossal cheek! And he wanted it all for love, I assume?'

'For free, Mother. Glen doesn't think in terms of love!'

'Then why on earth did you get involved in the first place?' Faith Marlow brushed back a lock of greying russet hair, and fluttered her eyelashes. 'Presumably his talents weren't confined to your kitchen.'

'Honestly, Mother! You sound like Lucy.' Sophie sniffed. 'And just for the record, *I* did the cooking in my kitchen. Glen kept his skills for the paying public.'

Sophie spent next day helping out at the garden centre, to free Charlotte for a haircut for the celebration meal Faith had booked at a hotel in Usk for a treat. Ben, Sophie was glad to see, looked relaxed and fit, and confirmed that life was good.

'With a wife like Charlotte, it can't fail to be,' he said with satisfaction.

'True,' agreed Sophie. 'Few men marry a landscape gardener who's a pleasure to look at, a great cook, and

probably wonderful at other things you'd rather not discuss with your baby sister.'

Ben laughed, and raked his bright hair back with a
grimy hand. 'All of that and a lot more,' he agreed. He
gave Sophie a long, level look. 'I'm a *very* lucky man.'

She nodded, blinking hard, then turned to the cus-
tomer waiting to pay for a load of spring-flowering
bulbs.

It was a peaceful, restorative weekend. After the delicious Sunday lunch Charlotte cooked in the familiar
house which had once been home to them all, Sophie
began the long drive back to Highfield Hall, assuring her
loved ones that she'd be back at Christmas.

'Though there's no reason why you can't come and
visit me, Mother—or you two, either, long before then.'

'We're shaping up for the festive season already, so
we'd have to leave it until the New Year,' said Charlotte
regretfully, giving Sophie a hug, 'but you must go,
Faith.'

'I may, at that, now Glen is out of the way,' said Mrs
Marlow, and kissed her daughter. 'In the meantime take
care of yourself, darling. And ring me the minute you
get in.'

After stowing boxes of wallflowers and bulbs in
Sophie's car, Ben kissed her and promised he'd bring
Charlotte up for a visit as soon as he could, and she
drove off at last, a lump in her throat as the trio stood
waving until she was out of sight.

When she arrived at Ivy Lodge Sophie rang her
mother, unpacked the car, and made coffee. And only
then listened to Glen's voice, which was no longer furious and threatening, but caressing and deliberately
husky in the way he considered irresistible. It had all
been one great mistake, he assured her. Now she'd had

time to think it over she must surely realise they were perfect for each other. Entreating her to call him back, he went on in the same vein until the tape ran out.

Her smile was cynical as she deleted the message. Glen really meant that for him someone with Sophie Marlow's training, skills and personal savings was perfect. But he was out of luck. Her savings were staying put. And if he needed skills like hers for his restaurant he would just have to pay for them.

The following week went by without a single sighting of Jago Smith, and Sophie tried to convince herself that this was a good thing. After doing her best to freeze him off right from the first, for the *coup de grâce* she'd insulted him to his face. So if he'd lost interest she had only herself to blame.

You mean congratulate, Sophie corrected herself, and went to her aerobics class in the village hall on two evenings, instead of one, enjoyed a meal at the Rose and Crown one evening with Jon Barlow, the Highfield bar manager, and otherwise worked so late she was glad to collapse with supper on a tray when she got home. When Saturday dawned fine and sunny she spent the morning tidying up in her small garden to prepare it for the bulbs and wallflowers Ben had given her. And in the afternoon, full of virtuous glow after her labours, she went shopping in Cheltenham, spent far too much on a new sweater, treated herself to two paperback novels, various delicacies from a chain store food hall, and went home to enjoy an evening spent in much the same way as Saturdays in the past. Because it was the busiest evening in the Highfield restaurant Glen had never been free. Which meant he'd monopolised her Sundays, and expected her to cancel any other arrangements if he had

time off unexpectedly in the week. Sophie shook her
head in wonder as she drove back to Long Ashley, finding it hard to believe, now, that she'd put up with him
so long. Never again. Next time she embarked on a relationship with a man—if she ever did—*she* would lay
down the ground rules.

Next day was fine and, after another hour or two in
her garden, the misty sunshine decided Sophie to walk
the couple of miles to Stephen and Anna Laing's home,
which was a large, rambling house with a paddock for
the pony shared by their eight-year-old twin daughters
Robyn and Daisy. Sunday lunch at the Laings' was just
the sort of occasion, Sophie decided, to wear the new
black sweater which flattered an upper half a little op-
ulent in its curves for her own taste. With the addition
of black high-heeled boots, and jeans in fawn cord which
clung to the hips her aerobics classes had improved over
the weeks, Sophie felt quite pleased with herself when
she set out.

By the time she arrived at End House she was rather
regretting the high-heeled boots, but the welcome she
received quickly eclipsed any ache in her toes. Robyn
and Daisy launched themselves on her the moment
Stephen opened the door, and were quickly followed by
a pair of black retrievers equally vociferous with their
welcome.

'Out!' commanded Anna Laing, hurrying from the
kitchen to release wonderful aromas of lunch along the
hall. 'Long time no see, Sophie Marlow. Welcome
back.'

Anna Laing was tall, with long fair hair like her
daughters, but, Sophie noted, returning her hug with enthusiasm, a great deal more rounded than usual.

Anna exchanged a conspiratorial grin with Stephen as

he took Sophie's coat, then beckoned to her daughters. 'Robyn and Daisy have news to impart.'

Since the twins were hopping up and down simultaneously, obviously bursting with excitement, Sophie laughed. 'I can see that. Right, girls. I'm all ears.'

'Mummy's going to have a baby,' they said in one voice, and Sophie gave Stephen a startled look as she hugged the twins.

'How wonderful,' she exclaimed, then gave a rueful smile to Anna. 'It really is a long time since I was here.'

'Anna wouldn't let me tell you until she was well over the danger mark,' Stephen apologised. 'I told you to come early so we could break the news and ply you with celebratory fizz before the others come.'

While the drinks were poured Sophie handed out books with a pony-riding heroine for the girls, chocolates and a bottle of Burgundy for her hosts. 'Though if I'd known I would have made it vintage champagne!'

'Ready and waiting on ice,' Stephen assured her triumphantly. 'I'll dash off and open your venerable red first to let it breathe in time for lunch—extravagant creature that you are.'

Anna Laing believed in serving food that could wait around happily while she enjoyed the company of her guests, and Sophie sat down with her on a sofa in the large, welcoming sitting room, realising how much she'd missed her visits to End House.

'Glen's gone, then,' said Anna, and patted Sophie's hand. 'Am I allowed to say good riddance?'

'You might as well! Everyone else has.'

'Including your mother, no doubt.'

Sophie nodded ruefully. 'She'd been trying her best to shape up for the role of Glen's mother-in-law, but just couldn't hack it.'

'Had you actually thought of *marrying* him, then?' demanded Stephen, appalled.

Anna laughed. 'Forgive him, love—he tends to be over-protective where you're concerned.'

Sophie grinned at her boss, secretly very touched. 'Don't worry. I never looked on Glen as husband material.'

'Thank the Lord for that,' he said piously, then went off to let in neighbours with a son the same age as the twins. The children ran off to the twins' room to play while their parents, well-known to Sophie, joined in the discussion of the impending arrival over their celebratory champagne.

'Twins again?' asked Nina Tracey.

'No, thank heavens.' Anna exchanged a look with her husband. 'It's only one baby this time, and we already know it's a boy.'

'At our stage in the proceedings it was all a bit of a surprise,' said Stephen rather sheepishly.

Andrew Tracy laughed, and slapped his back. 'Does the old ego good, though.'

'Not so much of the old,' protested his host, and went to answer the door again.

Sophie was so deeply involved in baby discussion that Stephen had ushered the new arrival into the room before she realised, with a great lurch in the region of her midriff, that the fourth guest was not the vicar, as was sometimes the case on these occasions, but Jago Smith, in the cord suit and black sweater of their last meeting, and bearing bottles and a bouquet of flowers.

'You know Sophie, of course,' said Stephen. He introduced Jago to Anna and the Traceys, relieved him of the offerings, and handed him a glass of champagne.

Anna thanked her guest, gave him a warm welcome

and her undivided attention for a few minutes as, un-selfconscious as always, she explained the reason for the celebration.

'Congratulations! It's very good of you to invite me,' said Jago, with such sincerity that Anna beamed on him, chatted for a while, then excused herself to see to the lunch.

Sophie jumped to her feet. 'I'll help.'

'No need,' said Anna, but after a glance at Sophie's face accepted without demur. 'On the other hand if you feel you must slave for me after slaving for Stephen all the week who am I to refuse?'

Sophie followed Anna from the room, a prey to a variety of emotions, not least of which was the knowledge that her choice of black sweater and pale cords echoed Jago's clothes so exactly she felt silly.

The dogs were outside in the garden with the three children, but inside, except for Sophie's inner disquiet, all was peace and calm in the big kitchen until Anna turned to her with a questioning eye.

'What's up? Don't you like Jago Smith?'

'He's charming,' said Sophie firmly, beginning to slice the loaf Anna pushed towards her.

'That's not an answer.' Anna crossed to the stove to shift a vast pot of soup to heat. 'Ewen asked us to look out for him, and an extra guest is never a problem for Sunday lunch, so this seemed the easiest way.' She waved an admonishing ladle. 'He wasn't invited to pair off with you, love, I promise.'

'I know that! Shall I make butter curls?'

'If you want to, by all means.' Anna eyed her curiously as she stirred. 'Look, do you know something sinister about the man that we don't, by any chance?'

Sophie shrugged. 'He's a perfectly respectable barrister with a sideline of writing books on legal subjects.'

'And that's all I'm going to get,' said Anna, resigned, and bent carefully to open the oven to check on the casserole simmering inside. 'Parsnips and leeks in the warming oven, so it's just the spinach to wilt and potatoes to mash.'

'You do the spinach; I'll do the potatoes.'

After the children were called in and served their lunch at the kitchen table Sophie went into the dining room to hand round steaming bowls of clear tomato soup fragrant with basil. When everyone was served she slid into the empty seat beside Andrew Tracey, noting that his wife Nina had taken on the job of entertaining Jago. And was finding it no hardship. Sophie had no problem either, since Andrew Tracey was a man with a wry sense of humour very much to her taste, and the meal was a pleasant social occasion she eventually had to admit was enhanced, rather than marred, by the presence of Jago Smith.

After helping Anna provide the children with the main course Sophie returned to the others to enjoy her portion of chicken casserole enriched with mushrooms, shallots, garlic, and a last-minute dollop of cream which blended all the flavours together.

'This is quite wonderful, Mrs Laing,' said Jago with reverence. 'Far better than my dinner over at the Hall the other night.'

'That's very kind of you—and do call me Anna. All the same, I hope the new chef is up to scratch.' She paused, pulling a face. 'Sorry, Sophie.'

'Don't be,' said Sophie, unruffled. 'And actually the new boy is good. Isn't he, Jago?'

'Very good,' said Jago, a flicker of surprise in his eyes

at a direct question from such an unexpected quarter. 'Sophie and I had dinner there together last week—quite by accident,' he added dryly, as interested looks arrowed at him.

'The restaurant was packed,' explained Sophie. 'I was with Joanna Trenchard, and she suggested Jago shared our table.'

'The meal was excellent,' Jago assured Stephen, 'so full marks to your new head chef.'

'That's a relief,' said Anna. 'I was never one of Glen Taylor's fans, but I have to admit he's a genius in the kitchen.'

'Let's see how he does in a kitchen of his own,' said Stephen with a malicious grin, and winked at Sophie as he left to provide the kitchen crowd with ice-cream.

By the time the grown-ups had consumed platefuls of hot citrus pudding, followed by wedges of crumbly local cheese and Anna's homemade oat biscuits, Sophie felt quite tired, and only too happy to relinquish her role of Anna's helper to Nina Tracey.

'I'll just take Andrew out to look at Dino for a minute,' said Stephen. 'We won't be long, Jago. I'll leave you in Sophie's capable hands.'

Jago leaned against the chimneypiece when they were gone, eyeing Sophie warily. 'If you prefer I can go out and look at Dino too. Whoever Dino might be.'

'He's the twins' pony. Andrew Tracey's the local vet,' said Sophie, and smiled a little. 'No need for a lawyer. Perhaps you could put a couple of logs on the fire instead.'

'Of course.' Jago turned his back on her and bent to poke the fire to life, then laid on more logs and tidied the hearth meticulously, making it plain that spinning out the task was a infinitely preferable to making polite conversation.

'It's all right, you know,' she said acidly. 'You're not obliged to talk to me.'

Jago turned round, shrugging. 'I was saving you the trouble of talking to *me*.'

She sighed. 'Look, I'm sorry for lashing out at you the other night. It was totally uncalled for and I apologise.'

To her surprise he came to sit down beside her, stretching out his long legs as he leaned back with arms folded. 'But you meant it,' he said sombrely, turning to look at her.

'One often says hurtful things in anger.'

'True. But I'm still at a loss to know why, exactly, I *made* you so angry.'

'Put it down to my temporarily jaundiced view of your sex.'

'Not quite all of them,' he said, surprising her. 'I saw you with the bar manager the other night.'

Sophie turned to him in surprise. 'Were you in the Rose and Crown? I didn't see you there.'

'I went for a run in the park last thing, and saw you arrive home.' He gave her a sidelong glance. 'I made myself scarce, before you could add spying to my unspecified sins.'

Sophie shrugged. 'Jon's a friend. Before Glen arrived on the scene I often went to a film or for a meal with him on his night off.'

'And now, of course, he's only too glad to renew the arrangement.' Jago got up quickly when Anna and Nina reappeared, the other men came back, and conversation became general while coffee cups and brandy were handed out.

Jago refused the brandy. 'It's only a short drive back, but I won't risk it, thanks.'

'Wouldn't do for an upholder of the law to be found over the limit,' agreed Andrew. 'I fleetingly considered the law myself when young.'

'Only because you fancied yourself in a wig and gown,' teased his wife, and smiled up at Jago. 'I bet you look impressive in yours.'

'Arcane custom,' Jago said, shrugging. 'Horsehair and a black stuff gown in a heatwave is no fun, I assure you.'

'How long before you apply for silk?' asked Andrew.

'A while yet.'

'Is that because you're too busy writing?' asked Anna.

'Not really. Some QCs are prolific writers as well as carrying on their legal careers.' Jago smiled. 'But at the moment I like my life the way it is.'

'Sensible man,' approved Andrew, and sipped his brandy with relish.

'You're on foot, Sophie, so how about a snifter for you?' said Stephen

'You know she doesn't like it,' said Anna. 'Have some more coffee instead, Sophie. You too, Jago.'

Suddenly there was a commotion outside and the twins burst in, with Alexander Tracey in close pursuit.

'Mummy, if we lend Alex one of our hats is it all right for him to ride Dino?' they said in unison.

'All right with you, Nina?' said Anna.

'Fine. From the look of my son a bit more mud won't do him any harm!'

'Sophie, will you come and watch us before Alex has a turn?' pleaded Robyn. 'We can go over jumps now.'

'Can you really? Of course I'll come,' said Sophie, getting up. 'Lead on, troops.'

'Just a trot around for you, Alex—no jumping,' warned his father.

'Take a jacket from the back entry, Sophie,' said Stephen, 'and don't let them keep you out there too long. It's cold.'

Outside in the paddock the wind was rising, and clouds were massing on the horizon. Sophie kept an eye on them while she watched the children and, with the dogs frisking at her heels, applauded each twin as they put Dino over a series of small jumps before Alex was given a hard hat and a leg up.

For a couple of circuits the pony trotted round the paddock obediently with a delighted Alex in the saddle, then heavy drops began to fall and Sophie called to the twins, who allowed Alex to ride back to the stable, then held Dino's bridle for him to slide off, grinning all over his face.

'Now you help us take Dino's saddle off and rub him down, Alex,' ordered Daisy, as she led the pony inside.

Sophie stayed to help, and once the pony was settled she went back into the house with her escort of children and dogs, where they were met by Jago at the back entry, brandishing towels.

'I volunteered to bring these while Anna made tea,' he explained, handing them out. 'I'll dry the dogs; I'm told the rest of you guys can cope on your own.' He smiled at Sophie. 'The leaves in your hair match it to perfection, by the way.'

When dogs and children were reasonably mud free the latter went off to play upstairs again, Sophie put her boots to dry near the stove, then visited a cloakroom to brush her hair free of leaves and renew her lipstick, and emerged into the hall to find Jago waiting for her with the dogs.

'How very nice of you to wait!' she said, surprised.

'I am nice,' he assured her. 'Some day I may even convince you of that.'

When they rejoined the others Stephen grinned as he looked at Sophie's black socks. 'You should have borrowed Anna's wellies.'

'Too big,' said his wife ruefully, and patted the sofa beside her. 'Curl up on here, Sophie. Nina's pouring. How did you enjoy the gymkhana?'

'I was impressed. Robyn and Daisy have come on enormously since I last saw them ride.' Sophie grinned at Nina. 'Alex looked very pleased with himself up on Dino.'

'Which means riding lessons, no doubt!'

After Sophie finished a second cup of tea, which Jago brought her, she got up, smiling regretfully at Anna. 'I really must go. The weather doesn't look too promising.'

'You can't walk back in this,' said Stephen from the window. 'It's pouring down out there.'

'I'll give Sophie a lift,' said Jago at once, and Anna smiled on him in approval.

'In that case neither of you need rush away.'

'I must get back to the grind,' he apologised. 'If Sophie doesn't mind leaving.'

'Of course not,' she said at once. 'I'll get my boots—'

'Stay there,' said Stephen, 'I'll fetch them.'

Jago expressed his thanks to his hosts, took his leave of the Traceys, and once Sophie was booted again helped her into her raincoat to race through the downpour to his car.

'Sorry to tear you away,' Jago said, as he switched on the ignition.

'A better alternative to hiking home through this lot,' Sophie assured him, and turned round to wave.

'You enjoy a good relationship with Stephen Laing,' Jago remarked.

'We worked well together from the start,' she agreed. 'It was good to see the girls again today. I haven't been to End House for ages. I've missed Anna's famous lunch parties.'

'Did Taylor enjoy them too?'

Her lips tightened. 'No. He went once, but we didn't go again.' The occasion had been a total disaster. Whereas Jago's addition to the guest list had been an instant success.

'From a bystander's point of view,' said Jago carefully, his eyes on the road, 'it seems that Taylor's departure meets with general approval all round. Does that include yours?'

'I thought you might have seen that for yourself firsthand,' she retorted.

He shrugged. 'Regrets might have crept in once you'd had time to calm down.'

'My only regret is letting him into my life in the first place.'

Jago gave her a sidelong glance. 'Then why did you?'

'Propinquity, mainly. I love my job and my house, but my social life here is fairly limited. Glen was in the same situation when he arrived on the scene, so after a while we started seeing each other occasionally.'

Due to the rain darkness had fallen so quickly it was only when Jago turned off the road into the estate that Sophie realised he'd taken the entrance to the Frasers' cottage instead of Ivy Lodge.

Jago left the engine idling outside the house. 'I was economical with the truth when I said I needed to work. I took you away from the Laings because I want you to come in for a drink and talk to me for a while. I'm determined to learn the mysterious secret.'

Sophie turned to look at him, but he stared straight ahead into the glare of the security lights. 'What secret?'

'Your reason for disliking me.'

'Hasn't anyone ever disliked you before?'

'Probably hundreds of people.' He turned to look at her. 'But you're the only one I care a damn about.'

Sophie felt the familiar, unsettling lurch in her midriff. 'It's nothing personal,' she said with constraint.

'I'd still like to know.'

She stared down at her hands, then sighed. 'Very well. But not here. My place.'

'Why?'

'If we talk here you'd feel obliged to walk me home afterwards.'

Jago looked at her steadily for a moment, then turned the car round and drove her home.

'Coffee?' she asked as she turned on the lights.

'No thanks.' Jago helped her off with her raincoat, then surprised her by taking her hands in his. 'Sophie,' he said, in tone which quickened her pulse, 'something tells me that I'm not going to like this secret. So before you cast me out into the figurative snow there's something I want.'

Sophie looked up at him in question, then caught her breath, her heart pounding as she realised what he meant. Then she was in his arms, his lips on hers in a hungry, open-mouthed kiss which lit up every erogenous zone she possessed. Her body melted against him and, instead of the suave, practised lovemaking she would have expected, Jago Smith's lips and tongue wooed hers with a primitive demand that sent hot delight rushing through her entire body as his hands coaxed it into startled response.

'I knew it,' he whispered against her mouth.

Her eyes stared up dazedly into his. 'Knew what?' she asked unevenly.

'How it would be to make love to you.' He held her fast as she stiffened in his arms, and laughed a little, deep in his throat. 'Just kisses, Sophie.' His eyes darkened, and she swallowed hard, then his mouth was on hers again and she leaned against him shamelessly, wanting the kiss to go on and on, knowing that when it was over reality would kick in. And none of this could happen again once the truth was out.

He let her go at last, and Sophie stepped back, chest heaving, her nipples taut in response when the turbulence drew his eyes like magnets. She flung away, face flaming, and went into the other room, busying herself by switching on lamps and drawing curtains. But at last her delaying tactics ran out, and she turned to face Jago, who stood very still in the doorway, watching her like a hawk.

'First, Sophie,' he commanded, 'before you let me into this sinister secret of yours, tell me one thing.'

'Yes.'

'Was the feeling mutual?'

She drew in a deep breath, then pushed the hair behind her ears and looked him straight in the eye. 'You know it was. Totally. I was attracted to you the moment I opened my front door to you. Even though your eyes were the only thing visible.' Her face shadowed. 'It was a shock the next day to find out who you actually were.'

'So we have met!' He moved like lightning to seize her hands. 'Where? When?'

Sophie looked down at the hands holding hers.

'We've never actually *met*, Mr Langham Smith. But I've seen you in your wig and gown. In an embezzlement case a few years ago.' She raised her eyes to his. 'My brother went to prison because you failed to get him off.'

CHAPTER FOUR

Jago dropped her hands as though they burnt him. 'To my knowledge, I've never defended a Marlow.'

'His name's Pritchard. Ben's my half-brother.' Sophie slumped down on the sofa, her shoulders drooping. 'He borrowed some money he couldn't pay back in time. Embezzlement, you lawyers call it. So he went to prison.'

'And where you're concerned I sent him there,' said Jago grimly. 'Does your brother hold me responsible for ruining his life?'

'No.' Her eyes met his. 'But for years I did.'

Jago eyed her in silence, brows drawn together as he thought back to the case.

'It was a while ago,' he said at last. 'But I remember him well. Probably because he pleaded guilty, and I never had a hope of getting him off. He was a very nice guy who, now I think back, looked a lot like you.' His mouth twisted. 'That's why I thought I'd met you before.'

'Probably. We both take after our mother.'

He winced. 'Does she hold me to blame too?'

Sophie shook her head. 'No. She blamed herself. Bitterly. After my father died she soldiered on alone to keep his market garden going. Eventually the bank started making noises about a loan she'd taken out to expand. Ben worked in the accounts department of an electronics firm at the time. When his boss was on holiday abroad Ben did some financial juggling to get the cash for her. But he couldn't keep the balls in the air long enough. His boss came back sooner than expected and found the deficit before Ben could pay it back.'

Jago stared at her, appalled. 'Good God—do you hold me responsible for the loss of the family business as well?'

'No. Because it wasn't lost. The sale of Ben's flat went through too late to keep him out of prison, but it kept the business afloat.'

He relaxed slightly. 'Does your mother still run it?'

'No. Ben does that now, with the help of his wife, Charlotte.' Sophie heaved a sigh. 'Ben's crime wasn't heinous, but it was nevertheless the crime of theft and false accounting. As you well know. It would have been impossible to get a job afterwards in his own line of work. When—when he came out he took over from Mother. Ben likes growing things. He'd always helped out in the nursery when he was at home, and he worked in the gardens at the open prison they eventually sent him to. So it wasn't too much of a transition. Except,' added Sophie sombrely, 'for having to fit back as an ex-con into a community where people had known him all his life.'

'How did his wife take it?'

'He met Charlotte for the first time after he came out. She was working for Mother, and knew the whole story before she ever laid eyes on Ben.' Sophie's lips tightened. 'Her parents did everything they could to prevent the marriage, but Charlotte refused to let Ben's past affect their relationship.'

'As it's going to affect ours,' said Jago heavily.

Sophie's eyes fell. 'You and I don't have a relationship.'

He moved swiftly, and took her hands to pull her to her feet. 'Ah, but we could have, Sophie.'

She made a half-hearted attempt to pull away, but he drew her hard against him and kissed her, igniting the same overwhelming response as before. He held her closer, his hand sliding down her back to pull her against him. She shivered at the touch of his hands under her sweater, felt the unmistakable demand of his arousal against her. Her breasts hardened in response to his caresses as their kisses grew fiercer, and at last he raised his head, his eyes blazing into hers. 'Do you need further proof?'

'No,' she gasped. 'Not that it matters.'

Jago held her by the shoulders, rubbing his cheek against her hair. 'It matters to me. Sophie, we could be so good together—'

'In bed, you mean?' she demanded.

He released her, thrusting back his dishevelled hair. 'Yes. But not exclusively. I meant in every way that makes a relationship work.'

'We hardly know each other—'

'Something time normally remedies.' His eyes stabbed hers. 'But you don't intend to allow that?'

She shook her head. 'If I have any kind of relationship with a man my family expect to know something about him, but where you're concerned that's out of the question.'

'So once I go back to London you'll forget I ever existed?'

'Oh, I doubt that! One way and another you're a hard man to forget, Mr Langham Smith.' To Sophie's dismay tears ran down her cheeks and she dashed them away impatiently.

'Sophie. Darling, don't cry!' Jago seized her in his

arms, but, utterly vanquished by the endearment, Sophie cried all the harder.

'Sorry, sorry,' she said hoarsely, and tried to push him away, but Jago held her fast.

'What exactly are you crying for?' he whispered.

'The moon, I suppose,' she said hopelessly.

He turned her face up to his. 'Does that mean what I think it means?'

'Probably.'

Jago drew her down beside him on the sofa. 'So if you and I had met as strangers, with no murky secrets in the past, you wouldn't be sending me away?'

'No,' she said thickly, and blew her nose. 'Not that there's much point in discussing it.'

He slid an arm round her waist and drew her close. 'Then we won't.'

The wind rather taken out of her sails Sophie twisted round to look up at him, and Jago smiled.

'I haven't given up the fight, Sophie Marlow. I'm merely applying my legal mind to find a way round the problem.'

'It failed with Ben's,' she said cruelly.

'Of course it failed! He pleaded guilty, and embezzlement always carries a custodial sentence, however short, so I couldn't keep your brother out of prison.' He brought her face up to his. 'And that, of course, is the crux of the problem. You can't see past that.'

'Do you blame me?' She pulled away and got up. 'To you it was just a case. But it cost Ben his good name, his job and his freedom. I hated the very sound of your name afterwards, Mr Langham Smith.'

Jago jumped to his feet, glaring at her. 'Then why the hell did you let me make love to you just now?'

Colour flooded Sophie's face. 'I didn't *let* you. It just

happened. Besides,' she said honestly, 'I don't hate you any more. As must be perfectly obvious.'

His eyes kindled as he moved towards her, but he shook his head when she backed away. 'Don't worry, Sophie. Unlike your friend the chef I won't use force to gain my evil way. But I'm only human, so don't look at me like that, either,' he added unevenly, 'or I'll be tempted to do something we'll both regret.'

'Would we regret it?' said Sophie rashly.

Jago moved to a safe distance. 'If there's no future in it, *I* would. So I'm taking myself off, while I still can.'

Sophie turned away in misery. 'Goodbye, then.'

Jago let out an explosive sigh and caught her in his arms again, his mouth hungry on hers and, for few brief, heart-stopping moments, they were united in a fever of physical longing so intense that when Jago released her at last Sophie desperately wanted to hang on to him, plead with him to stay.

'This is torture,' he said roughly.

She nodded her head in mute agreement. 'I just wish…'

'So do I!'

They looked at each other in silence for a moment or two, then Jago turned on his heel, strode from the room and out of the house.

Sophie sank down on the sofa, her body throbbing with Jago's lovemaking even while her mind grappled with the fact that he was the last man in the world she should have fallen in love with. *Love?* She thrust her hands through her hair. Was this burning, yearning feeling really love, or just a longing for something she couldn't have? She stayed where she was, huddled in misery, until the chime of her doorbell brought her to her feet to race into the hall. Jago had come back!

But when she threw open her front door her radiant smile died at the sight of Glen Taylor, in city suit and new, fashionable haircut.

He brushed past her and shut the door behind him. 'Hello, Sophie. I thought I'd come and see how you were getting on without me.'

'Very well, thank you,' she said dully, burning with disappointment.

'I don't believe that. You miss me. Admit it.' His hot blue eyes probed hers. 'I went up to the Hall to find out if you were away, and Joanna told me you were at the Laings. So I hung about with her most of the afternoon, then I came round here to find a strange car outside. I thought your lawyer friend would never leave.'

'You're wasting your time, Glen. I meant it when I said you're not welcome here.' Sophie went to the door, but he caught her wrist and held her fast.

'Let me go,' she snapped.

'Not until I've had my say.' His grip tightened, but his eyes were suddenly pleading. 'Sophie, I know I've gone about things in the wrong way. I suppose I just went mad at the thought of losing you. You know how I feel about you.' He smiled triumphantly. 'If you like I'll even marry you.'

'You must be joking!'

He stared at her incredulously. 'You're turning me *down*?'

Sophie nodded. 'That may be hard for you to grasp, Glen, but, yes. I'm turning you down. So let me go, please.'

Angry colour flooded Glen's face, but she willed herself to stay calm as she backed towards the hall table.

'But I asked you to marry me,' he repeated blankly, as though he couldn't believe his ears.

'And I'm refusing.' Sophie tried to detach herself but Glen's fingers bit into her wrist, and suddenly she saw red. 'Let me go right now or I'll call the police,' she threw at him.

'You wouldn't do that!'

Sophie reached for the phone with her free hand but he snatched it from her.

'No, you don't.' He jerked her into his arms, but Sophie dodged away in such open disgust Glen's temper flared out of control.

'Still playing hard to get, you cold little fish. But I'll make you respond to me once, if it's the last thing I do,' he panted, and thrust a hand into her hair to keep her head still as he ground his mouth into hers. Fighting mad now, Sophie ducked away and made for the sitting room. Glen caught up with her, and pulled her down on the sofa, but Sophie yanked herself away with such violence she landed on the floor, hitting her cheek-bone against a small table *en route*.

'Sophie!' gasped Glen in consternation, and dived to pick her up, but she shoved him away in fury and got to her feet, relief flooding through her when she heard hammering on the front door.

'*Sophie!*' shouted Jago. 'Let me in.'

Sophie slapped away Glen's helping hand and raced to the door, quelling an urge to hurl herself into Jago's arms as she opened it. 'I've got a visitor,' she gasped, waving a hand towards her sitting room.

Jago cast a hard, all-encompassing look at her dishevelment. 'What the hell's going on? Are you all right?'

She nodded valiantly. 'Fine.'

'I doubt that.' Jago strode into the sitting room to confront Glen Taylor. 'You again,' he said, his face like thunder. He exchanged a look with Sophie. 'Has this person harmed you in any way?'

'I didn't hit her,' said Glen defensively. 'She hurt her face when she fell.'

'Fell?' Jago spun round to face Sophie, his eyes on the reddening mark on her cheekbone. 'Is he lying?'

'No.'

'Tell me exactly what happened,' he ordered.

'I fell off the sofa.'

'It was an accident,' Glen repeated, backing away.

'Not so fast,' growled Jago. 'I don't like the sound of this. Sophie, what's Taylor doing here?'

'He came to propose,' she said baldly.

Jago's eyes slitted. 'And?'

'I refused. Glen didn't believe me. We had an argument.'

'During which you fell off the sofa and hit your head?' said Jago, and turned on Glen, fixing him with eyes like steel blades. 'It's my belief, Mr Taylor, that Miss Marlow is lying. That you assaulted her. And in the process of trying to defend herself she suffered an injury for which you are responsible.'

'You've got it all wrong, Jago,' said Sophie hastily. 'It was a complete accident.'

'And I'm a complete fool,' said Glen bitterly, looking from Sophie to Jago. 'I see it all now. You're a hell of a sight more than just Sophie's lawyer, *Mr* Smith.' He gave a derisive laugh. 'The best of luck to you, mate. She's a frigid little piece—'

Jago started towards him, murder in his eyes, but Sophie could take no more.

'No. Just *don't*,' she ordered. 'And you, Glen, make yourself scarce. Now! Jago, see him out, please. I—I don't feel too good.' She fled to the small cloakroom at the back of the hall. Eventually, deciding she wasn't going to be sick after all, she washed her face, leaned against the wall for a moment to compose herself, inspected the bruise and went to the kitchen for a pack of frozen peas to hold to her cheek.

'Has he gone?' she asked Jago, when he came after her.

'Damn right he's gone. Now tell me the truth. Did the bastard try to rape you?' he demanded.

'Of course not, nothing remotely like that. He was just trying to bring me round to the idea of marrying him.' She tried to smile. 'He came all dressed up in his best suit to propose, too. But Glen didn't hit me, Jago. I really did fall off the sofa—'

'But you *were* fighting to get free of him?'

'Stop cross-examining me,' she said crossly, shifting the peas a little. 'My face hurts.'

Jago eyed her grimly. 'It's a good thing I came back.'

'True. But why did you?'

'I had a feeling something was wrong. Which it was.' He took her hand. 'I could have beaten the living daylights out of Taylor just now.'

She smiled wryly. 'But your legal training counselled prudence.'

Jago scowled. 'He escaped a battering by a hair's breadth, believe me.'

'I do. But I don't think he'll come back again,' said Sophie, devoutly hoping she was right.

His hand tightened on hers. 'As I said before, I can get the court to issue an injunction against him. Or first of all,' he added, with sudden inspiration, 'maybe I'll get Charlie to write him a letter.'

Sophie stared up at him blankly. 'Charlie?'

'Charles Langham Smith, Solicitor. My kid brother.

He can send your Mr Taylor an official letter advising him to keep away from you, with indications of worse to follow if the idiot bothers you any more. Darling, what's the matter?' added Jago abruptly, eyeing her pallor.

'Suddenly I feel a bit off,' said Sophie apologetically, and tried to smile. 'I'd better go to bed.'

Jago took her hand. 'Can you make it upstairs on your own?'

'Of course I can.'

'I'm not so sure. I'd better stay until I know you're safely tucked up. I can let myself out.'

'Thank you,' she said gratefully. 'Sorry to be so feeble.'

Jago waited in the hall while Sophie negotiated a staircase which had suddenly assumed the proportions of Mount Everest. When she reached the landing she held up a thumb in shaky triumph.

'Made it! I'll do the bathroom bit first, then I'll get into bed. You can go now, if you like. I'll be fine.'

He shook his head. 'You're suffering from shock, Sophie. What do you say to some tea once you're settled in bed? I won't trespass in your bedroom a minute longer than necessary.'

Seized by the desire to have him stay there all night, Sophie smiled ruefully round her impromptu ice-pack. 'I would like some tea,' she admitted. 'Thank you.'

Feeling grubby after the episode with Glen, Sophie would have given much for a long, hot shower, but settled for a hasty wash and some ferocious teethbrushing instead. When she emerged from the bathroom, minus the frozen peas, she listened to the rattling of cups down below, her eyes wistful at the hint of intimacy. With a sigh she got into pyjamas and dressing gown, brushed her hair gingerly, then left the door wide open and got into bed to wait, propped up against pillows, for Jago to arrive.

When he appeared in the doorway she smiled at him. 'I'm going to have a black eye.'

'Quite possibly,' he agreed, setting a tray down on her bedside table. 'How do you feel?'

'My face is throbbing a bit, but otherwise I'm fine now I'm in here,' she said firmly, and looked at the tray. 'Just one cup? Aren't you going to share my tea?'

He smiled wryly. 'I waited to be asked.'

'Then I'm asking.' Sophie looked at him in appeal. 'Stay for a while, Jago? Please.'

'Of course I will.'

When Jago came back with a cup he brought a packet of biscuits. 'I thought you might fancy one of these.'

Sophie considered the idea. 'I do. Thank you.'

Jago filled the cups and put a couple of biscuits in Sophie's saucer, then looked round for somewhere to sit.

'Perch on the bed,' Sophie advised. 'My little cane chair would never hold you.'

But Jago leaned against the brass rails at the foot of her bed instead, and eyed her searchingly. 'Are you sure I shouldn't call a doctor, Sophie? You might be suffering from concussion.'

'Certainly not! My face hurts a bit, but after a night's sleep I'll be fine.' She smiled brightly. 'It's very good of you to stay. The kitchen's exactly the same as yours, of course, so it wasn't difficult for you to find everything. But I apologise for the embarrassing scene again. Not something you bargained for when you went to lunch with the Laings today—'

'Sophie,' he interrupted. 'Stop chattering. If my presence is making you nervous I'll go.'

'*No*. Please don't do that! At least not yet.'

Jago smiled. 'You know perfectly well that I'll stay as long as you want. In fact,' he added, 'I hate the very thought of leaving you alone at all tonight.'

'I'll be fine,' she said, without much conviction.

'My idea,' said Jago drily, misinterpreting her tone, 'was to sleep on the sofa downstairs.'

Sophie looked him in the eye. 'If you are going to stay, there's a perfectly good bed in the spare room.'

Jago's face stilled. 'I think the sofa might be wiser.'

'Afraid I'll walk in my sleep?'

'It's more likely I might.'

'The sofa's not very big.'

'But it's farther away from you.' He got up. 'Maybe it's best if I go back to my place, after all. You can always ring if you need me.'

'Fine,' she said, and put her cup back on the tray, her disappointment so intense she wanted to cry.

'What is it?' he said quickly. 'Do you feel ill?'

'No. Not ill. Just a bit nervous, I suppose,' she muttered, refusing to look at him.

'Then I'll stay,' he said decisively. 'Try to sleep, Sophie, and if you still feel seedy in the morning tell Stephen you're taking the day off.'

She smiled meekly. 'Thank you, Jago. Goodnight.'

He bent to kiss her undamaged cheek. 'Goodnight. If you want anything just whistle.'

When she was alone Sophie lay picturing what would happen if she did. Her imagination ran riot, conjuring up scenes where Jago came running and seized her in his arms, a prospect which made Sophie restless, and sleep impossible. In the small hours, when a visit to the bathroom finally became an urgent necessity, she slid out of bed stealthily and tiptoed along the landing to the bathroom in the dark. When she emerged she ran full tilt into Jago, who scooped her up as she stumbled.

'Are you ill?' he demanded.

'No,' she said, as he carried her back to bed.

'You're shivering,' he said tersely, thrusting her under the covers. 'Where can I find a hot-water bottle?'

'I'm not cold,' she said unevenly, and stared up at him. 'You're shivering, too.'

'But not with cold, either, so I'd better go, before—'

'Before what?'

With a groan Jago hauled her into his arms, just as she'd imagined he would. 'I was a fool to stay here. I might have known what would happen.'

'Nothing's happened yet,' she said, her voice muffled against his shoulder.

'Only because I'm hanging on to every scrap of will-power I possess.' He laid her back against the pillows and sat looking down at her with such unconcealed need Sophie's eyes snapped shut.

'I'm sorry,' she muttered. 'It's my fault.'

'Your fault?'

'I wasn't nervous.' Her lashes rose on eyes heavy with guilt. 'I only said that to make you stay.'

Jago smiled, a look of such blazing male triumph on his face Sophie's heart turned over. 'I wasn't leaving you anyway, darling. I'd give a lot to come in there with you and hold you in my arms all night. But if I did I'd want to make love to you. And you're just a little fragile, so I'm not going to. At least,' he added, his voice deepening, 'not tonight.'

CHAPTER FIVE

THIS time when Jago left her Sophie fell asleep almost at once, and woke groggily in the first grey light of day to find him at her bedside.

'How do you feel?' he whispered.

She yawned, and pushed the hair out of her eyes. 'I'll let you know when I wake up. How did you get on with my sofa?'

'Not too well. I abandoned it for the floor at some stage, but now I'm off, Sophie.' He kissed her good cheek fleetingly. 'I suppose it's too much to hope that you're taking a day off?'

'Much too much.'

He frowned. 'In that case make sure you finish early, or at least on time. I'll come round tonight and see how you are.'

The promise was the only thing which kept Sophie going all day. She arrived in her office too late for personal talk with Stephen, other than a brief explanation of her black eye, and the day grew busier and more exhausting as it went on, until Stephen finally emerged from a meeting to put his foot down, insisting she went home at once.

'Why the devil did you come in with a shiner like that? I could have managed without you for one day.'

'It looks worse than it is,' she assured him. 'I've mustered all the heads of departments for tomorrow, by the way. Nine-thirty sharp.'

'Are you up to taking the minutes?'

'Behind dark glasses, of course I am.' She smiled at him. 'I haven't had a chance to say how much I enjoyed lunch yesterday. It was so good to see the twins again. I've sent a note to Anna. Great news about the baby.'

He grinned. 'Bit of a shock at first, just between you and me, Sophie. We thought we'd finished with nappies long since.'

'The twins seem thrilled.'

'By the *prospect* of a baby brother, yes,' he said ruefully. 'Maybe the reality will have less appeal.'

'Is Anna keeping well?'

'She was a bit sickish for the first couple of months, but she assures me she's feeling good now.' Stephen looked at her questioningly. 'She liked Jago Smith, by the way. So did I. But we thought you seemed a bit put out when he arrived. Do I take it you disagree with the majority vote?'

'Not at all,' she assured him. 'He was a great help in seeing Glen off last night.'

'Handy having a barrister on tap.' Stephen smiled slyly. 'Particularly one who is not, shall we say, immune to your charms, Miss Marlow.'

'See you tomorrow,' she said, laughing, and went to collect her coat.

When she was halfway home her mobile phone rang.

'Time you finished for the day,' said Jago sternly.

'I'm on my way across the park right now.'

'Just as well. I was coming to get you.'

When Sophie reached her front gate Jago was waiting for her.

'How do you feel?' he demanded, taking her briefcase.

'A bit tired, but otherwise not too bad,' she assured

him. 'See?' she said, as she switched on the lights in her hall. 'The bruise is fading already.'

Jago shut the door behind him and kissed the face she held up for inspection. 'I should have blacked Taylor's eye for him to compensate,' he said with deep regret. 'Have you anything planned for this evening?'

She pretended to think. 'It's one of my nights for aerobics, but in the circumstances maybe I'll give it a miss.'

'Wise decision, because I've organised dinner for two at my place.' He smiled. 'Will you join me, Miss Marlow?'

Sophie felt such a gush of pure happiness her answering smile dazzled him. 'I'd be delighted, Mr Langham Smith. Just give me time to shower and change. If the meal requires your attention I'll follow you later.'

'No way. I'll wait here until you're ready,' he said firmly. 'And tomorrow night ring me when you're ready to leave and I'll collect you—'

'No,' she said quickly.

His eyes narrowed. 'Why?'

'Highfield is a tight little enclave, where everyone knows everything about everyone else.' Sophie looked at him in appeal. 'If we're seen together everyone would assume you'd taken over from Glen.'

'Fat chance of that,' he said grimly, 'in our situation.'

'Don't!' She put her hand on his arm. 'When do you actually leave here, Jago?'

'Weekend after next. I'll be finished with the book by then. I'll stay with Charlie while I look for a place of my own.'

'Couldn't you have stayed with your brother to write?'

Jago laughed. 'At the time, no. But the current girl-friend is current no longer, so I'm given the freedom of his spare room for a while.' He took her in his arms. 'But I shall be living here on your doorstep for the best part of two weeks yet, Miss Marlow. Why?'

She leaned against him. 'I lay awake last night, thinking—'

'So did I!' he said with feeling. 'But go on. What were you thinking?'

'Although a long-term relationship is out of the question for us,' she began slowly, 'we could see something of each other while you're here. If you like.'

'I like half of that very much indeed,' he said, and kissed her, taking his time over it. 'This seeing each other,' he muttered against her mouth. 'Does it include this?'

'Oh, yes,' said Sophie recklessly, and, having burned her boats, found the strength from somewhere to push him away. 'Go and read, or something, in the sitting room while I get ready.'

Jago traced her lips with a caressing fingertip. 'Whatever you say. Shall I put some of these lights out, or do you always leave them on?'

'Normally, no.' She pulled a face. 'But recent events have made me a bit edgy. I didn't fancy coming home to a dark house tonight.'

'Surely Taylor wouldn't have the gall to put in an appearance again after last night?'

'Probably not. But I feel wary just the same.'

Jago scowled. 'Perhaps the message winking on your phone is an apology from him. If not it should be!'

'I doubt it.'

She was right. It was Lucy, proposing the week after next for a weekend together.

'Old friend?' queried Jago, leaning in the doorway.

'We were at school together,' said Sophie. 'We've

both been roped in as bridesmaids at a friend's wedding. We're going shopping with the bride.'

He frowned. 'So you'll be away the weekend I leave.'

'Afraid so.' She turned hurriedly, pushing the thought away. 'And now I *must* get out of this suit. Shan't be long.'

Sophie rushed through a shower, pulled on a honey-coloured sweater with the cord jeans, slid into flat shoes for once, disguised the bruise with foundation and high-lighter, decided it was a waste of time to bother with lipstick, and rushed downstairs to find Jago in the hall, tapping his watch.

'I was very quick!' she said indignantly.

'Remarkably so compared with others I've known.'

'Namely, Isobel?' she said sweetly.

'And others before her,' he said, so smug Sophie dug him in the ribs, and he retaliated with a kiss which went on for so long only the unromantic rumbling of her stomach reminded him that he was taking her home for dinner. Which, he told her, as they walked hand in hand, consisted of a cold roast chicken sent over from the Highfield kitchens during the afternoon.

'My instinct was to order a three-course dinner for two, complete with caviare and champagne,' said Jago, as he hung her coat on a peg in the Frasers' hall, 'but Joanna Trenchard might have been curious. I thought maybe you wouldn't care for that.'

'How right you are! I have to work here after you're gone, Mr Langham Smith.' A shadow crossed her face at the prospect, and Jago pulled her close.

'But I'm here now. So are you. Let's enjoy what we have.'

'What exactly do we have?' she asked, tilting her head back to look at him.

'I can only speak for myself,' he said softly, his eyes gleaming under lowered lids. 'But at this moment in time everything I want is right here in my arms.'

'Likewise,' she whispered, and reached up, her lips parting as his mouth met hers.

It was a long time before Jago let her go. When he raised his head at last he smiled crookedly. 'We're still in the hall.'

'So we are,' said Sophie, blinking owlishly. She smiled at him. 'What are we going to eat with this chicken?'

Jago confessed that his culinary skill extended only as far as new potatoes with parsley and butter, and a bowl of salad leaves Sophie took over to toss with lemon juice and olive oil.

'For pudding Joanna insisted on including one of the cherry pies the pastry chef made for tonight,' Jago informed her, as they sat down to eat at the small round table by candlelight. He grinned. 'I had the feeling she was angling for an invitation to share my dinner.'

'I'm sure she was,' said Sophie tartly. 'Ever since our surprise dinner party she's been asking elaborately casual questions about you each time I run into her.'

'And what have you told her?'

'I disclaimed all knowledge of your personal life,' she said loftily, but her eyes danced. 'I felt it was a bit risky to say you'd just broken off a long-standing relationship. Joanna might have come steaming in to offer you consolation.'

He grinned. 'I might have welcomed that.'

Sophie stared at him, arrested. 'Would you?'

The grin vanished. 'You know damn well I wouldn't. For one thing I'm not in need of consolation where

Isobel's concerned. And even if I were, yours is the only consolation I want, Sophie Marlow.'

She shook her head in wonder. 'Amazing, isn't it?'

'What, exactly?'

She looked at the angular, handsome face, the errant lock of dark hair falling across his forehead above the intent, possessive grey eyes. And wondered how on earth she was to get on with her life once Jago Smith was no longer part of it. 'You. Me. This,' she said at last.

He reached across the table to take her hand. 'Not so amazing from my point of view. One look at your bare pink feet that first night, Sophie Marlow, and I was done for. And just to set the record straight,' he added deliberately, holding her gaze, 'discounting the usual hormonal crushes when young, I've never been in love before.'

Sophie gazed at him, dumbfounded. 'Not even with Isobel?' she said at last.

'No. We had common interests and enjoyed each other's company, but that was it.' Jago smiled wryly, his hand tightening on hers. 'I never had the least inclination to go slaying dragons for her as I do for you. I was ready to kill Taylor with my bare hands last night.' He released her hand to let her get on with the meal, his eyes questioning on hers. 'How often have you been in love, Sophie?'

'I've had relationships, but I've never felt like this before.' She looked at him levelly. 'It's the last thing I wanted to happen. But it has, Jago. As you know very well.'

He jumped up and held out his hand. 'Come here.'

'What for? I thought I was getting cherry pie,' she protested, but she went anyway, touched when he was careful with her bruise as he smoothed her head against him. 'Or did you have something different in mind for dessert?' she muttered against his chest.

'Certainly not!' he said virtuously. 'My only thought was to make coffee while you stretch out on the sofa in there. I shall bring the pie in with me.' He tilted her face up to his. 'You look delectable, but a bit shadowy round the eyes, even under the good one, Sophie.'

'It was hard going today,' she admitted, and let him lead her into the other room.

'Take your shoes off and recline seductively with that hair spread out against Rosanna's blue cushions,' he said, his eyes devouring her as she obeyed. 'Back in a minute.'

While he was gone Sophie came to a decision. If two weeks of her life were all fate allowed with Jago Smith then so be it. She would relish every minute, with no regrets for what could have been, only joy in what she had, right here and now in the present. The future could wait.

When Jago came back with a tray he put it down on the end table beside her, and sat on the edge of the sofa to look into her face. 'Disturbed night or not, I got on remarkably well with the book today,' he told her. 'I should be finished by the end of the week.'

Sophie went cold. 'After which there'll be no reason for you to stay on here,' she said, looking away.

Jago hauled her up against him and planted a hard, admonishing kiss on her mouth. 'Except for a very pressing reason, right here in my arms.' He laid her back against the cushions and smoothed her hair back from her face. 'I'm due in court on Monday week, I was informed today, by my tyrant of a head clerk. But until then, as far as the rest of the world is concerned, I'm still hard at it on my book.'

'So you'll be here for a whole week with nothing to do,' said Sophie, her mind working overtime.

'Precisely.' His eyes bored into hers. 'In fact, I could be on a beach, or beside a pool somewhere, soaking up some sun before my winter of discontent sets in.'

'Discontent?'

'What else can it be,' he said grimly, 'if you insist on letting the past put paid to our future?'

But Sophie wasn't listening. She was occupied with thoughts of her lover lying beside some foreign, sun-drenched pool, while she was labouring away in the depths of rain-drenched Gloucestershire. Lover? she thought, startled, and Jago, homing in on her surprise, put a finger under her chin.

'What mind-blowing thought struck you just then?'

'That I'm due some time off.'

'Then you'll come with me!' Jago's eyes lit with a look which brought her up into his arms, rubbing her good cheek against his. 'Are you sure about this? Because if you do come,' he added huskily, 'there'll be no question of separate bedrooms.'

Sophie nodded. 'Absolutely sure.'

Jago crushed her close, then let her go. 'Have some of this pie while we talk options.'

Sophie pulled him back as he made to get up. 'I don't really want any pie. At least not right now.'

'Neither do I.' His eyes gleamed. 'If I told you what I really want you'd probably take to your heels.'

A faint smile played at the corners of her mouth. 'So walk me home, then.'

'Right *now*?'

'Yes.'

'Why?'

'Because I do my own housework, Mr Langham

Smith, while you enjoy the services of the wonderful Angela.'

Jago eyed her blankly. 'I've lost the plot somewhere. Why should Angela send you running for home so early?'

Sophie shrugged. 'To be blunt, I'd rather make it my place, not yours.'

'Ah!' Comprehension flared in Jago's eyes. 'You think Angela might be suspicious if she detects perfume on my sheets.'

'Or anywhere else.'

'Right!' said Jago, and pulled her to her feet. 'To-morrow we'll eat at your place. No more time-wasting.'

'I'm seeing you tomorrow, too?' she asked, smiling, as he wrapped her in her coat.

'And every other day.' He hurried her through the door. 'And, fear not, I'll make sure Angela never knows you crossed my threshold.'

'Good thinking,' said Sophie, shivering as a chill wind rustled the trees into eerie shadows in the torchlight.

Jago held her close on the short walk back to Ivy Lodge. 'A bit different from the first time we did this,' he said in her ear. 'I was suffering from frostbite all the way to your place.'

'I had to try!'

'To hate me?'

'To keep you at arm's length, Jago. I knew from the first what would happen if I didn't. And it has,' she said simply.

Jago stopped to kiss her, then hurried her up the path to Ivy Lodge. He took her key and unlocked the door, closed it behind them, and turned to Sophie in the narrow, enclosed space.

'Would you like coffee?' she said breathlessly.

He shook his head, the look in his eyes lighting bonfires deep inside her. 'No coffee. I just want to hold you in my arms all night.'

'I'm not sure about *all* night. You'll have to leave before it's light.'

Jago threw off his jacket, then unbuttoned her coat with fingers made clumsy by need. Breathing rapidly, he took her hand and hurried her up to her bedroom, where Sophie kicked off her shoes and pulled her sweater free, but he stayed her hand.

'No. Let me,' he ordered, and very slowly peeled the sweater up over her breasts and smoothed it over her head.

Sophie's shivering increased when he slid down the zip of her jeans and laid her on the bed to ease them off, leaving her in briefs and bra he removed very slowly, sliding the silk from her skin, his eyes molten with a heat which sent Sophie burrowing under the quilt when she was naked, her flushed face buried in the pillow.

Jago tore off his own clothes, then he slid into bed and turned her in his arms, sliding his hands down her back as he kissed her, his tongue seeking hers in a caress which set her body on fire. She felt him grow hard and throbbing against her and thrust her hips against him, glorying in his response as he bent his mouth to her breasts. Sophie shivered at the touch of cool lips and hot, enticing tongue, and thrust herself against him, gasping when streaks of flame shot through her as he teased erect, sensitive nipples between his fingertips. Jago slid down further in the bed to kiss the smooth, satiny skin of her waist and stomach, and she gave a low, ragged moan as first his fingers, then his seeking tongue coaxed her to the very brink of climax. In a frenzy of longing she arched her back, and he surged upwards between her parted thighs and plunged them both into a maelstrom of sensation which left Sophie limp in his arms at last as the throbbing pangs of it died away.

Jago turned on his back eventually and held her close. 'I told you how it would be,' he said, his voice husky with satisfaction.

'Fantastic?' she said drowsily.

His arms tightened. 'Is that how you'd describe it?'

'It was for me.'

Jago breathed in deeply. 'Likewise, my darling.' He raised his head to look down into her heavy eyes. 'I forgot about your face. Did I hurt you?'

Sophie gave him a slow, glittering smile. 'I didn't notice.'

He smoothed her hair back from her face. 'You're very good for my male ego, Miss Marlow.'

She fluttered her eyelashes. 'It all depends, Mr Langham Smith, on one's definition of good.'

He laughed and kissed the demure smile on her lips. 'Are you tired?' he added abruptly.

'Not tired exactly.' Sophie thought about it. 'In fact, not tired at all.' She stretched luxuriously, elated as she felt his body stir instantly against hers. 'I feel wonderful.'

'You certainly do,' agreed Jago gruffly. 'So if you do that again, prepare for consequences.'

'You mean you might want to make love to me *again*?'

'No might about it. But I'm not going to. At least not yet.'

'When then?'

'I was going to say after we've had some champagne

to celebrate, but the bottle I had ready is sitting in the Frasers' fridge,' he said ruefully. 'Once I knew what you had in mind I forgot everything in my hurry to rush you back here.'

'Including the cherry pie,' she reminded him.

'I'll bring it over tomorrow night.'

'Don't forget! In the meantime, let's talk travel.'

'Right,' he said, pulling her close. 'Where do you fancy?'

'Somewhere sunny, and not too far away so we waste time getting there. And I must be back by Friday week,' she reminded him. 'Can you arrange that at such short notice?'

'I'll do my damnedest, Sophie.' Jago ran his fingers through the strands of vivid hair on his shoulder. 'My vote goes to a villa with a pool—but no maid—and total privacy for one glorious week. Italy, or Portugal, maybe.'

'I don't mind where it is,' said Sophie, her eyes lambent at the prospect. 'I'll break the news to Stephen in the morning.'

'Will he be surprised?'

'Probably. I'll tell him I need a holiday to get over the unpleasantness with Glen.'

'He'd be surprised to know I'm going with you!'

Sophie pulled a face. 'He wouldn't be the only one. So could you leave a day or two beforehand, Jago? Tell Stephen you've finished the book earlier than expected? I'll take the coach down to Heathrow and meet you there.'

Jago's face shadowed. 'So you can return here after the holiday and pretend I never existed.'

'Don't!' Sophie shivered, and burrowed her head

against his shoulder. 'Let's just be happy in the present, Jago. Please?'

Jago turned her in his arms to look down into her face. 'Make me happy, then.'

'How?' she whispered.

'Improvise,' he said very softly.

'Like this?' She slid her hands down his spine, her fingers tantalisingly hesitant as they glided slowly round his waist, then ventured lower to discover whether she was making him happy.

And found she was.

CHAPTER SIX

AFTER taking off from Heathrow through driving autumnal rain they arrived in Lisbon to find it basking in sunshine. At the airport Jago picked up the hire car he'd arranged and, with Sophie navigating, they drove south on a short, leisurely journey through the pines and olive groves of the Arrabida peninsular to search for the Quinta Viana, which Jago told her was somewhere deep in the woods near Azeitao.

'Which is literally "the little place of olives",' Sophie reported in delight from her guidebook.

They found the house eventually, after a perilously steep ascent up a paved drive with a grass mule track running through it, and emerged into a large garden full of palms and cypresses which enclosed the *quinta* in complete seclusion. And, unlike the modern villa-with-pool of the holiday brochures, it was an old, one-storey building with shuttered windows, and weathered gold walls girdled by a veranda.

'Jago, it's heavenly,' breathed Sophie as she got out of the car. 'How on earth did you manage to find *this*?'

'Through a friend,' said Jago, putting his arm round her. '*Quinta* means farm originally, but these days it applies to any big house with a fair bit of land attached. I wanted something special for you, darling, so after lots of frantic telephone calls and e-mails while you were working, eventually it was all arranged. I didn't tell you before in case it didn't come off—ah, this must be the caretaker.'

A smiling, elderly woman emerged from the far end of the house to welcome them, and introduce herself as Senhora Fonseca. She handed over the key, and informed them, in heavily accented English, that she had left basic supplies in the kitchen, as instructed, and would be back to collect the key the following Friday. She gave them directions to the local market, wished them a pleasant holiday, and went off on foot, leaving them to explore the house on their own.

After the heat of the afternoon the house was cool. On the veranda elderly rattan chairs flanked a table with a fat candle in a bronze holder with a glass shade. Louvred doors led off into rooms containing only a bare minimum of furniture made of wicker and dark, carved wood, with beautiful *azulejos*, the famous blue and white tiles of Portugal, on the walls in the kitchen and bathroom.

'*Azulejo* is an Arabic word meaning smooth, nothing to do with azure blue as I thought,' said Sophie, consulting her guidebook again.

'But, picturesque though it is, it's the *only* bathroom,' warned Jago.

She smiled at him. 'No matter. We take turns. Or share.'

'I'll look forward to that!' He kissed her quickly. 'Choose which room you want and I'll bring in the luggage.'

Beforehand, though eager to make the trip with Jago, Sophie had suffered secret qualms about sharing a house and a bed for a whole week with a man who, madly in love with him though she was by this time, was not only someone she'd thought of for years as the enemy, but a man she'd known for only a perilously short time. But when they unpacked together in a cool, shadowy room with a large tester bed, the entire process with Jago seemed so comfortable and natural they could have been sharing such intimacies for ever.

'What are you thinking?' he asked, sitting on the bed to watch her brush her hair.

'I was a bit worried about this before we came,' she said honestly, and smiled at him over her shoulder.

'Committing yourself to me for a whole week?'

Sophie nodded. 'But not now we're here in this serene old house, Jago. Surely it's not a holiday let?'

He shook his head. 'It's the second home of a Lisbon banking family. My chum knows the Alvares family and persuaded them to let us stay here.' He got up and took her in his arms. 'So here we are. For one whole week. Will we last the course without coming to blows?'

They had to, thought Sophie. No point in wasting precious time in quarrelling. 'I'm *very* easy to get on with,' she said firmly, and reached up to kiss him. 'I'm also very hungry. Let's inspect these supplies.'

In the cavernous kitchen a modern cooker, refrigerator and electric kettle had been added to the original cupboards and wood-burning stove. A garland of garlic bulbs hung on a hook on the wall beside a ceramic container of salt, and bread and goat's cheese had been left on the big square table, accompanied by a flask of olive oil, a vast bowl of luscious ripe tomatoes, and a bottle of local red wine.

'Probably the oil's from local groves as well,' said Jago, as he attacked the big, crusty loaf.

Sophie drizzled some of it on two hunks of bread, rubbed them with a clove of garlic, squashed a ripe tomato on each, seasoned them liberally from the salt container, and handed a slice to him. 'Try that.'

'Fantastic,' said Jago, tasting it.

'There's butter if you prefer,' said Sophie, inspecting the contents of the fridge as she munched. 'Milk too, and eggs. And there's coffee and sugar in this cupboard, and,' she added, with a smug little smile, 'I brought my own teabags.'

'Clever girl. I knew there was a good reason for bringing you along!' Jago grinned, and kissed the mouth she opened in protest. 'My friend gave me a list of places to eat. Do you fancy dinner out tonight?'

She shook her head. 'If you'll settle for an omelette and the red wine I'd rather stay in. We'll go shopping in the local market tomorrow and eat grilled sardines in the sunshine somewhere for lunch.'

'Done!' He grinned at her. 'And, tempting though the sharing idea is, I'll let you read alone in the tub tonight. But don't stay away from me too long.'

Sophie had no intention of wasting time alone in the bath that night. After only a few minutes she went back along the veranda to find Jago in one of the reclining chairs, the candle alight inside its glass holder.

'How romantic!'

He got up to bow, and gestured at the sky. 'I've even organised a moon. Do I get a reward?'

Sophie soon found that the kiss she gave him was a mistake when he discovered she was naked under her dressing gown. 'No,' she said breathlessly, pushing away his invading hands. 'Your turn in the bath while I dry my hair, then I cook dinner.'

'Yes, ma'am!' he said smartly, planted a last kiss on her mouth, then left her alone with her racing pulse.

Although she'd chosen to stay in, Sophie took time over her appearance. She put on a clinging shift in apple-green cotton jersey, high-heeled sandals, applied a minimal amount of make-up, and brushed her hair until its disparate streaks of brown and gold and amber melded together into molten copper.

When Jago, towel-draped, joined her in the bedroom he looked at her in silence for a moment. 'You look sensational.' His eyes gleamed with unmistakable purpose as he moved towards her, but she backed away, shaking her head.

'Dinner!'

'Even though I could eat you instead, high heels and all?'

'Even so,' she said, and gave him a stern glance over her shoulder as she strolled from the room. 'Don't be long.'

Although they'd spent every minute possible together until Jago left for London two days before, tonight, knowing they had an entire week together in the privacy of this beautiful old house, the surroundings added a subtle new dimension to their relationship. They sat side by side, as close together as possible, at the big scrubbed table while they shared the tomato salad and vast cheese omelette Sophie had cooked, their pleasure in each other's company a living presence in the room.

'Food for the gods,' said Jago, scouring his plate with a hunk of bread. He gave her a sidelong scrutiny. 'It's a shame no one else can see how beautiful you look, but I'm glad we stayed here tonight.'

Sophie smiled up at him. 'I made the effort to please you, Jago, no one else.'

'Thank you, my darling.' He raised her hand to his lips and kissed it. 'To show my appreciation, I'll do the washing-up while you sit out there on the verandah and commune with the moon.'

'How lovely,' she said with a sigh as she got up.

'Some men I've known look on washing-up as a threat to their male charisma.'

'If they do,' said Jago scathingly, 'they don't have any to start with.'

'Unlike you,' she told him, and dodged away, laughing.

Alone for a moment in the moonlight, Sophie looked out over the shadowy, rustling garden and tried to crystallise the moment, to hold it in her mind as something to look back on when... She brushed the thought away. 'When' could wait until she was forced to deal with it. 'Now' was all that mattered.

'Penny for them,' said Jago, letting himself down beside her in one of the ancient, creaking chairs.

'I was just thinking how unreal this garden looks in the moonlight, enclosed in the trees. We're shut away in our own enchanted world.'

'An arrangement which meets with my enthusiastic approval, Miss Marlow. No pool, of course, but I can live without one. Especially,' he added, with a lascivious grin, 'if I can share your bath with you.'

Sophie eyed the long legs stretched out in front of him. 'Would we both fit in together?'

'Of course we would. We're a perfect fit in every way, my darling.'

They were, too, she conceded, feeling the familiar tug at her heartstrings. Jago Langham Smith was the first man she'd ever met who suited her in every possible way, intellectually and physically.

'You're very quiet.' He reached out for her hand.

'I was just thinking how right you were.'

They sat in harmonious silence for a while, but at last Jago let out a deep, unsteady breath and turned to her. 'Darling, it's no use. I've existed for two whole days

without you. I can't wait a minute longer. Come to bed.'
He got up, pulling her gently to her feet, and with a
smile which made it plain she was in complete agreement Sophie took his hand and led him to the room
chosen for their own.

In complete silence Jago undressed her with caressing
hands by the moonlight streaming through the windows
on either side of the louvred double door. But when they
were naked together in the dark, carved bed at last, instead of the urgency Sophie had expected, he hung over
her looking down into her moon-silvered face.

'Tell me you've missed me,' he said, in a tone which
made her shiver.

'You know I have.'

'Show me how much.'

Sophie reached up, her hands sliding into his hair as
she brought his face down to hers to kiss him, and at
the first touch of her lips Jago abandoned all control and
began to make love to her with a desire made all the
more intense by their brief parting. Sophie's response
was equally ardent, fuelled by the knowledge that all too
soon this fiery glory would be only a memory to look
back on. She gave herself up to the touch of his hands
and lips and, at the last, surrendered herself to him with
such utter abandon Jago kept her locked in his arms long
after the last pulsing throes of their passion had died
away.

'Mine,' he said hoarsely at last, and moved a little to
hold her close in his arms, one leg imprisoning hers in
such fierce possession Sophie was seized by a sudden
need for him to know the truth.

'I never made love with Glen,' she said gruffly, and
felt Jago stiffen in surprise.

He sat up, turned on the light, and piled pillows

against the carved wood of the bed. He propped her against them, then pulled up the covers and lay on his stomach, looking up at her.

'No wonder he was like a tiger baulked of his prey! Why not, Sophie?'

'I wasn't in love with him.' She thrust her hair behind her ears and met his eyes with candour. 'As must be obvious to you, I've had a physical relationship with a man before. It didn't last long.'

'Why did it end?'

'I got the Highfield job.' Sophie looked down at him, smiling wryly. 'We'd been students together, and we both went to London to work after university. It was no grand passion, Jago, so when our lives veered in different directions we agreed to call it a day. Paul and I are still friends, and when I go up to stay with Lucy, the three of us often have an evening out together.'

'But you've been at Highfield for four years, darling,' said Jago slowly.

'Yes. But no one's shared my bed at Ivy Lodge—until you did.'

Jago slid up to seize her in his arms, holding her so tightly she made a smothered, laughing protest.

'Just expressing my gratitude,' he said impenitently.

'Glen liked people to think he was my lover,' she went on, when she could. 'It was always the bone of contention between us. In fact,' she added thoughtfully, 'it's probably what drove him to propose in the end—he thought I was holding out for a wedding ring.'

'If he turns up again,' said Jago grimly, 'I shall take great pleasure in informing him that he hasn't a hope in hell. You're mine, Sophie Marlow.'

'You know that's not possible—' she began. But Jago cut her words off with an obliterating kiss, and she was lost again in a rising tide of desire that blotted out everything other than the need to merge herself, heart and soul, with the man who made such spine-tingling verbal love to her she was in a fever of longing by the time she was engulfed in waves of fulfilment he watched her experience first before he collapsed on her in the throes of his own release.

From the first they were united in the desire to make the most of every minute of their time together. Each morning they woke in each other's arms to the sheer joy of being together, made luxuriously slow, unhurried love, then shared a bath and dressed together. Afterwards they drank fruit juice on the veranda in the cool early sunshine, then walked down to the market in the village to buy fruit and cheese, and fresh hot rolls for breakfast.

Later on they did a little leisurely exploring by car, lunched on the promised grilled sardines on the beach at Portinho da Arrabida most days, then returned to stretch out on the veranda chairs, content to laze the afternoons away together. In the evenings they went off into Azeitao or Palmela for a more sophisticated meal. And dined very early by local standards so they could return to the Quinta Viana and their bed. But they rarely slept until the small hours, and lay awake in each other's arms, preferring to savour the precious, fleeting minutes than waste them in sleep.

Sophie learned that Jago's parents lived in Norfolk, where they'd bought a house after his barrister father retired, and Charlie, the younger son, had a flat in Notting Hill. In return, she told Jago about her own family, that Ben's father had died when he was little, and her mother had married again a couple of years later.

'My dad owned a garden centre and the house that

went with it,' said Sophie. 'It's where I grew up, but Ben and Charlotte live there now. Mother has a tiny flat in a renovated country house, and I have my own little retreat at Highfield.'

'I'll always be grateful to Ewen for letting me have his place there,' said Jago fervently, and kissed her nose. 'Fate obviously intended us to meet, Sophie Marlow.'

The first, inevitable shadow fell on the last morning when they were packing to leave.

'We never did come to blows,' said Sophie, doing her best to be cheerful, despite a heart like a lead weight inside her. 'Verbal ones, not physical, of course.'

'Probably because we avoided the one burning issue that would lead to them,' said Jago, and left his packing to take her in his arms and kiss her. 'So,' he said, looking down at her with a confidence which rang alarm bells in Sophie's head. 'Now you've brought the subject up at last, darling, you can't really mean to leave me without a backward glance once we get to London?'

She gazed at him in anguish. 'But you know the answer to that, Jago. I made it clear from the start.'

His eyes narrowed ominously. 'You're telling me that after everything we've shared this week you're still determined on that?'

'I don't have a choice!'

'Even though you've told me, repeatedly, that you love me?'

'I *do*.'

'But you love your family more.'

The bleakness of his tone cut so deep Sophie detached herself and hugged her arms across her chest against the pain of it. 'Not more, Jago, just in a different way.' She met the wintry grey eyes in appeal. 'What we had together this past week was so wonderful it was unreal. I never dreamed I could feel like this about any man—'

'Thank you for that, at least!'

'There's no ''at least'' about it,' she contradicted, and breathed in deeply. 'The thought of saying goodbye today is tearing me to pieces, Jago. You must know that.'

'Then why the hell say it?' he said with sudden violence. 'Why can't we go on seeing each other?' He seized her by the elbows. 'Tell your family about me and let them make their own decision, Sophie!'

'How can I possibly tell them I'm seeing the man responsible for sending my brother to prison?'

They stared at each in silence which lengthened to such hostile, unbearable proportions that in the end Jago released her so abruptly Sophie stumbled.

'I did *not* send your brother to prison. But I assume I take that as a no,' he flung at her, and returned to his packing.

Sophie gazed wretchedly at his taut back for a moment, then zipped up her suitcase and began tidying the room.

'You don't have to,' snarled Jago. 'Cleaning's included in the price.'

Doggedly, Sophie went on stripping the bed in silence, and after a while Jago picked up their cases and went out to stow them in the car.

After the constant exchange of conversation of the previous few days the silence in the car was unbearable to Sophie when it became obvious that Jago had no intention of breaking it on the journey to the airport. When they approached Lisbon by the Ponte 25 Abril, the great bridge over the River Tagus, she gazed blindly at the city on its various hills, the famous Tower of Belem like a toy far below, but felt too miserable to appreciate the beauty of any of it. This unhappy ending to the fairytale had been inevitable all along. And she knew very well if Jago had been prepared to wave goodbye without a backward glance she would have been hurt. But in a very different way from this raw, gnawing anguish.

When they reached the airport there was the minimum of exchange between them over the mechanics of getting through the formalities, but once they were in the departure lounge silence fell again, and this time Sophie took out a book and tried to read. The print danced in front of her eyes, as meaningless as words in a foreign language, but she made herself turn the pages at intervals, determined to keep up the act.

On board the plane things were marginally easier when drinks and food trays were distributed, but afterwards Sophie sat staring out of the window, no longer even pretending to read, her heart heavy as she thought back to the excitement and pleasure of the flight out. By contrast the return journey was pure endurance, and once they'd arrived at Heathrow, after what seemed like several hours instead of two, they passed through Customs, still locked in silence, and Jago took charge of the luggage and made for the queue for taxis.

'I'll drop you off before I go on to Charlie's place,' he said tersely.

Sophie made no reply. Having been silent for so long, she couldn't have trusted her voice even if there'd been anything to say. Had it really been worth it? she wondered as they stood waiting. The week with Jago had been heaven, just as she'd imagined it would be. But the present hell was her reward for refusing to face the stark reality of their return to earth. After their week-long total rapport, in bed and out of it, she had never dreamed that her passionate, tender lover would transform into this cold, remote man who seemed to have fallen out of love with her so suddenly she found it hard to believe he'd ever felt anything for her at all.

'Where?' said Jago, as a taxi drew up beside them at last.

Sophie supplied the address of Lucy's flat and got in, tucking herself in the corner, as far away as she could from Jago. 'I hope this isn't taking you too much out of your way,' she said politely.

'Not at all,' he returned in kind. 'Charlie lives in Notting Hill.'

Something he'd already told her, Sophie remembered too late.

'Will your friend be home at this time?' he asked as the driver crawled through Friday rush hour.

'Probably not. But I have a key.'

When they arrived, Jago picked up her suitcase and got out, holding out his hand to help her out of the taxi. Sophie took it for the briefest moment possible then, in consternation, saw Jago pay off the driver and remove his own luggage.

'I'll ring for another taxi after I've seen you inside,' he told Sophie with finality.

Sophie rang the bell marked 'Probert', praying Lucy would be home early for once, but there was no answer.

'I'd better let myself in.' Sophie unlocked the main outer door under the pillared portico. 'Lucy lives in the basement flat. I can manage now, thank you.'

'I'll see you safely inside,' insisted Jago, and followed her down the stairs.

Sophie unlocked Lucy's door and switched on lights, touched to find that the flat was unusually immaculate, even to a vase of fresh flowers on the table. 'Do come in,' she said politely, and crossed to draw curtains across a window which looked out on steps ascending from a small paved area to the street.

Sophie turned to face Jago, wishing quite desperately he would go, but he stood his ground.

'Sophie.' He dumped down the luggage and moved towards her suddenly, his face hardening when she backed away. He took out his wallet and extracted a card. 'This is Charlie's address and telephone number.'

Sophie frowned. 'Why should I need that?'

His jaw tightened. 'If you change your mind you can reach me there.'

'But I won't change my mind, Jago,' she said in sudden desperation. 'I can't. You knew that all along.'

'But fool that I am,' he bit back at her, 'I didn't believe it. I was so bloody sure that our week together would change your mind.'

'I don't have a *choice*!'

'Of course you have a choice.' He moved suddenly, and seized her by the shoulders.

She shook her head miserably, and looked up into his tense face. 'If the position were reversed, Jago, would you take me home to your parents and expect them to welcome me with open arms?'

His hands tightened. 'Yes, I would. And if they didn't I'd live with that. As long as I had you.' His eyes stabbed hers. 'Which means I care for you a hell of a sight more than you care for me.'

'That's not true,' she retorted hotly. 'Besides, you're dealing with theory. I'm faced with fact.'

Jago's hands dropped and he moved back, his face like a mask. 'And the fact of the matter, Miss Marlow, is that for a little fling in the sunshine I filled the bill well enough, but now we're back to reality that's it. Over

and out.' His mouth twisted. 'Maybe I feel sympathy for
the jilted chef, after all.'

'That's not fair! There's no comparison—'

'If you mean I'm unlikely to come chasing back to
Highfield to plead with you, true enough. So just for old
times' sake—' Jago seized her in his arms, kissing her
so hard her head reeled when he thrust her away. 'I wish
to God,' he said, his voice plumbing new depths of bitterness, 'that I'd never laid eyes on you.'

CHAPTER SEVEN

SOPHIE stood rooted to the spot, staring at the closed door through a haze of tears, then jumped out of her skin when the door flew open and Lucy rushed in like a whirlwind.

'Sophie? What's up?' She dumped down a paper sack of shopping, threw a vast tote bag on a chair, and yanked her friend into an all-enveloping hug.

'Hi, Luce. Sorry for the long face.' Sophie sniffed hard, and smiled ruefully at her friend. 'I'm not sure if I just did something sensible, or made the biggest mistake of my entire life.'

Lucy raised an eyebrow. 'Would it be something to do with the man who shot past me at the street door? Tall, tanned, and *very* angry?'

Sophie nodded mutely.

'Sit down again,' ordered Lucy, shrugging off her coat. 'I'll make tea, and while we drink it I demand to hear all.'

Lucy Probert was the same age as Sophie, had been to the same schools and the same university, but otherwise she was very different. Tall, with dark, glossy hair cut short in the latest, high-maintenance style, she was striking rather than pretty, and for the past three years had provided invaluable assistance to the managing director of a property search company in the West End.

They were seated opposite each other at the table in the bay window, with tea and pastries in front of them, before Lucy, after giving Sophie breathing space by regaling her with the highlights of her day, fixed searching blue eyes on her friend's face.

'Now, then. The man I saw was carrying luggage. Was *he* the mysterious friend who whisked you off to the Algarve?'

Sophie nodded despondently, not bothering to correct her friend. Arrabida or Algarve, it made no difference now.

Lucy refilled her beaker, and pushed the plate of pastries towards Sophie. 'I went to enormous trouble to find your favourites, so eat one. And tell me about the mystery man.'

Sophie took a tiny strawberry tart and bit into it obediently. 'He was just someone who came to stay at Highfield. As a lot of men do. Only this one was—special.'

'*Extra* special if you took off on holiday with him. Just like that.'

'Exactly. And now he's back in his life here, and on Sunday I'll go back to my life there.' Sophie held out her cup for a refill. 'It was always understood that it was just for a week.'

'Are you sure *he* understood? He stormed past me like a force nine gale.' Lucy's eyes narrowed. 'He's not married is he?'

'Certainly not,' snapped Sophie, offended.

'Sorry, sorry! Then I take it he wants to prolong the idyll? If idyll it was.'

'It was. And he does. But it's out of the question.'

'Why? Is he a bank-robber, or something?'

'No.' Sophie hesitated, then, because she'd always told Lucy everything, gave her the truth. 'This is strictly between you and me, Luce. He's a barrister. And not just any old barrister. He's the one who defended Ben.'

Lucy choked on a mouthful of cake. 'The man you once wanted to murder?' she gasped.

'With my bare hands,' agreed Sophie. 'Until he turned up at Highfield not so long ago.' She gave her friend a wry little smile. 'When I fell madly in love with him instead.'

Lucy gazed at her speechlessly. 'Of course you did,' she said at last. 'Otherwise you'd never have gone off with him. I take it,' she added delicately, 'that you shared a room?'

'And sometimes a bath. And all night and every night a bed. Which, as a point of interest, are things I never did with Glen.'

'I *thought* you had more taste than that,' declared Lucy, unsurprised. 'But never mind Glen, what happens now with Mr X?'

'Nothing.' Sophie smiled sardonically. 'He's not exactly ideal to take home to meet the family is he? So it's over. And now you know why Mother thinks I went off on holiday with you.'

'Oh, glory, so she does. What tangled webs we weave, and all that.' Lucy frowned. 'Not even a word to the bride?'

'Especially not to the bride!'

Tamsin Hayford was the third member of the trio, and came from the same village, but from a very different family background. Which made no difference to the friendship. She'd attended the same playgroup, nursery and primary school as the other two, and had only taken off—unhappily—to the academic, single-sex school of her father's choice when she was eleven. Motherless from birth, Tam had been welcomed into both of her friends' homes like an extra daughter, and had earned

Sophie's undying gratitude by rushing to be the first to welcome Ben home from prison.

'Tam, according to Mother,' said Sophie, 'is floating around on a pink cloud, so I'm not going to spoil anything for her if I can help it. Even,' she warned, 'if she wants us to wear baby-blue taffeta with frills.'

Lucy shuddered. 'Surely she won't expect that?'

'It's no use trying to second-guess Tam. Who knows what she has in mind? And her father's paying for the dresses, so we'll just have to grin and bear it, whatever she chooses.'

'Last I heard, Tam was thinking of gold brocade for her wedding gown,' said Lucy pensively.

'No!' Sophie managed a real smile for the first time since her friend had arrived. 'It *might* work.'

'Tam won't care if it doesn't,' said Lucy, chuckling. 'She's happiest in riding breeches anyway. But she'll probably be here at the crack of dawn tomorrow, so we'd better get to bed reasonably early. What do you fancy for supper? Eat out, order in, or I could rustle up an omelette—?'

'*No!*' said Sophie, so vehemently she coloured when her friend stared. 'Sorry, I'm off omelettes. But I'd prefer to stay in.'

'Right,' said Lucy, regrouping hurriedly. 'I've got pasta, bacon and tomatoes and so on. Do you feel up to making one of those pasta bakes of yours?'

After graduating Sophie had shared the Bayswater flat with Lucy, which meant it was no chore to set about making a meal, as she'd so often done before, nor to take up residence in the spare room that had once been her own. After Sophie's departure for Highfield Lucy had found a replacement flatmate for a year or so, but these days earned enough to live there alone.

'Which,' said Lucy, as she tucked into the meal later, 'is so much better for my social life. If I bring the man of the moment home for supper, or whatever, he isn't put off by someone else's knickers drying in the bathroom, or run-ins with a fright in heated curlers in the morning.'

'I never did any of that,' protested Sophie, able to laugh by this time.

'No. Those were dear Tara's drawbacks.' Lucy smacked her lips appreciatively. 'And, unlike you, she was a rotten cook.'

When Sophie was in the bath later Lucy burst in without knocking, her eyes wide with excitement.

'Out! You've got a visitor.'

Sophie's eyebrows shot to her hair. '*I* have? Who?'

'He says his name's Smith. Otherwise Mr X!' Lucy grabbed a robe from the back of the door and held it out, shaking it like a matador. 'Up you get.'

'*No!*'

'What do you mean, no?' Lucy fixed her with a stern blue eye. 'Come on. Face the music, Sophie. It's you he wants, not excuses from me. I'll hide in my room.'

'But Luce—'

'But nothing. Out!' repeated her friend.

Still raw with hurt at Jago's parting shot, Sophie took her time to dress in jeans and a sweatshirt, left her hair in the untidy knot she'd tied on top of her head, and, not even bothering to look at her shiny face, left the bathroom and marched along the short narrow hall to the living room Jago had left only hours earlier.

He was standing by the table, looking haggard, and so much the stranger in a formal dark suit Sophie's angry greeting died on her lips at the sight of him.

'I'm sorry, I seem fated to get you out of the bath,'

he said stiffly, dragging his eyes away from her bare feet. 'I found your passport with mine when I got to Notting Hill. It seemed best to bring it round rather than trust it to the post.'

'I see.' Sophie gave him a long, cold look. 'How kind of you to bother.'

'Not kind,' he said with barely controlled violence. 'I wanted to see you.'

'Why?'

'Where's your friend?'

'Taking cover in her room.'

'So you could be alone with me? Did she think you wanted that?'

'It was more a case of Lucy wanting that. You were lucky to find us in,' she added.

'True,' he agreed, still standing motionless. 'Even luckier that your friend answered when I rang. You, no doubt, would have told me to get lost.'

'I hope my manners are better than that,' she retorted.

Sophie was still standing just inside the door to the little hall, so that when Jago did move at last she had nowhere to go when he closed the space between them and seized her shoulders, his eyes blazing down into hers. 'I just can't let you *do* this, Sophie. I can't believe that our week together meant nothing more to you than a holiday fling. I'm in love with you. And unless you're the most accomplished actress outside Hollywood you feel the same about me. Admit it!'

Sophie stared at him with hostility as his fingers bit into her shoulders, but the lie she was about to utter was silenced by a kiss of such overpowering sweetness she gave a stifled little sob and yielded to his urgent arms.

The buzzer on the door brought them both back to

earth with a bump, and Sophie tore herself away to lift the receiver.

'Sophie? Paul, here. Lucy said you'd be in tonight.'

'Hi, Paul,' she said hoarsely, and pressed the release button for the street door. She turned to Jago, pushed at the hair snaking down from the makeshift knot, tried to think of something to say, failed, shrugged hopelessly, and went to knock on Lucy's door.

'Paul's on his way down. You'd better come out.'

Lucy emerged warily. 'You OK?'

'No.'

When they went into the living room together Jago appeared to be in full command of himself again.

'Time I was on my way to fetch my brother—my parents are here for the weekend. We're meeting them for dinner,' he informed them.

'Thank you for bringing my passport,' said Sophie woodenly, and, with a quick look from one tense face to the other, Lucy went to let Paul in.

Jago tore his eyes from Sophie's face when Lucy brought Paul Radley in to be introduced, then studied the newcomer's face closely as they exchanged pleasantries. 'I'm afraid it's hello and goodbye,' he apologised soon afterwards, and turned to Sophie. 'Perhaps you'd see me out?'

With two pairs of riveted eyes watching, Sophie had no option.

'When do you go back?' Jago asked, when the door closed behind them.

'Sunday.'

'So this is goodbye, then.'

'Yes.' Though by this time Sophie was by no means as sure of it as she had been. The interlude in his arms had shaken her resolve badly.

'Is Radley the Paul who was your lover?' Jago asked abruptly.

She frowned blankly, then shrugged. 'He was.'

They stared at each other in brooding silence which grew more unbearable with every passing second.

'Sophie, for the last time, change your mind,' he urged at last, in a tone that cut her to the heart.

'You know I can't *do* that,' she said, her voice cracking.

His face hardened. 'Then I'm damned if I'll ask again. I spend my working life pleading in court, but otherwise I'm no good at it.' He paused expectantly, but when she said nothing his face set into a hostile mask. 'Oh, to hell with it. I just can't take this, Sophie. Goodbye.'

For the second time in hours she let him go, and in misery watched him mount the stairs, sure he'd turn at the top. But Jago Langham Smith strode out of her life without a backward glance.

CHAPTER EIGHT

LUCY opened a bottle of wine and served Paul with the warmed-up remains of the pasta bake, instead of going out for a meal as he'd expected, and Sophie, after a session alone in her bedroom to knock herself into shape, did her best to take part in the kind of evening the three of them had enjoyed so often before.

Paul earned a salary at his City bank that even a successful barrister like Jago Langham Smith would have respected, and as usual he was dressed in expensive casual clothes, his fair hair styled as skilfully as Lucy's. They made a prosperous looking pair, thought Sophie fondly, watching them sparring together.

'So who's this Smith guy, Sophie?' asked Paul at last, as she'd known he would.

'A friend.'

'Pretty close friend! He'd been kissing you *very* thoroughly before I arrived.'

'How do you know that?' demanded Lucy.

'Sparing your blushes, Luce, I have been in a position to know exactly what she looks like in such circumstances,' he said, grinning at Sophie.

'Not for years, you haven't,' she retorted.

'Was it a kiss and make up?' asked Lucy hopefully.

Sophie ground her teeth. 'It was a kiss goodbye. Now, can we *please* talk about something else?'

It was late when Paul left, and a lot later before Sophie went to sleep. The memory of Jago's last words stayed with her so forcibly she tossed and turned until the small hours, only to be woken from a heavy, post-dawn sleep by hammering on the door.

'Up you get, sleepyhead,' shouted Lucy. 'I've made breakfast.'

'I don't want breakfast,' groaned Sophie, hiding under the pillow, but Lucy came in and ruthlessly yanked it away.

'Come on. Tam's been on the phone. She'll be with us in an hour, to sweep us off to Knightsbridge.'

'Oh, all right,' sighed Sophie, and staggered out of bed, yawning.

'Breakfast first, you can dress afterwards. We're trying on frocks, remember, so I hope you packed some heels.'

Sophie gave her friend a look of scorn. 'Of course I did.'

'Mr X seemed totally fascinated by your bare feet last night.' Lucy patted her shoulder. 'He's a pretty impressive bloke, love. Isn't there some way you can get round the problem?'

'He wasn't impressive when it mattered most to Ben,' snapped Sophie, and shut herself in the bathroom.

Feeling better after the coffee Lucy had ready, Sophie apologised for her early-morning grumpiness. 'I couldn't get to sleep.'

'No wonder. The atmosphere was electric between you and Mr X,' said Lucy. 'Talk about striking sparks off each other—even your hair was crackling.'

'Which is more than it's doing this morning,' said Sophie glumly, and looked at her watch. 'I must do something with it. I suppose we'd better dress up a bit. I had the forethought to pack a suit,' she added.

'Amazing, in the circumstances,' said Lucy wryly. 'If

I'd been flying off to romantic places with a "friend" like Mr X I doubt I'd have been so organised.'

'Could you please shut up about him?' Sophie snapped, then bit her lip. 'Sorry, Luce.'

'My fault.' Lucy got up to clear away. 'Apparently Tam stayed in town with her parents-in-law-to-be last night, which is why she's so early. Probably glad to escape. But she's dossing down with us for the hen-night after the shopping spree.'

Sophie chuckled. 'Three females, a pizza and a bottle of bubbly. Not everyone's idea of a hen-night.'

'Tam isn't like anyone else,' said Lucy, laughing.

But for once Tamsin Hayford looked remarkably conventional when Sophie opened the door to her a few minutes later. Also remarkably svelte.

After all the hugs and kisses, and the rush to get back in the waiting taxi, Sophie looked Tam up and down in admiration when they were on their way. 'You look pretty gorgeous, bride-to-be.'

'You mean I look thinner,' said Tam, grinning. She gave Sophie a close scrutiny in return. 'So do you. But I've been rushing round organising my own wedding, keeping to a starvation diet, and sweating on a treadmill so I look like a dream to David when I drift up the aisle. What's your reason?'

'She's just sent the man in her life packing,' said Lucy.

'You mean it's over with Glen?' said Tam happily. 'Hurray.'

'You're out of date, dear. It's the one after Glen.'

'Wow,' said Tam with awe. 'I am out of touch. Tonight, Sophie Marlow, I want every last detail. Well,' she added on consideration, 'possibly not *every* detail.'

At one time the contrast between the three friends had

been marked. Lucy had always been tall and lean, Sophie short and curvy, and Tam, somewhere between the two in height, fought a constant struggle with her weight. Now, as the three of them left the taxi to search every floor of Harvey Nichols for the perfect bridesmaid dresses, Lucy and Sophie both in pricey tailored suits they wore to work, and Tam in a long navy blue coat with an emerald velvet scarf draped round her shoulders, the three of them drew more than one admiring look as they began their search.

'Right, comrades,' said Tam happily, 'we start at the top and work down, then we go back to the top to eat lunch. My treat.'

Sophie firmly pushed all thought of Jago from her mind, and entered into the spirit of things with almost as much enthusiasm as the other two when she found that taffeta and frills were the last thing on Tam's mind.

'Sophie's hair colour is the thing to watch,' said the bride-to-be, eyeing the mouth-watering creations on display. 'We need to work round that, though it won't be a problem, because practically any colour suits you, Luce.' She grinned at her friends. 'Dad told me to spend what I like—just this once.'

Although sorely tempted by a sequinned, leopard-print number which brought laughing protests from her friends, Tam was forced to abandon it for something more conventional when she found there was only one.

'Honestly, Tam!' said Sophie. 'Imagine the vicar's reaction if Luce and I sashayed down the aisle in something like that.'

'Rather fun, though,' said the bride regretfully, 'and perfect for the dance in the evening. The wedding breakfast's at home, of course, which is such a squeeze most of the guests are limited to the hop in the village hall.'

'By the way,' said Lucy casually, 'did you decide on gold brocade in the end, Tam?'

'No fear. I soon abandoned that idea for conventional cream satin, like anyone else, though I did fall for a few golds beads scattered here and there on the bridal bosom, now it's diminished a bit. I shouldn't look too bad.'

Since of the three of them Tamsin Hayford was the only one whose face aspired to actual beauty, her friends smiled at her indulgently.

'You'll look wonderful,' Sophie assured her. 'David's a lucky man.'

'So he says,' said Tam contentedly. 'Now, come on, I want you two to look wonderful, too. Downright gorgeous, in fact.'

In creations with labels they normally couldn't aspire to they could hardly fail, they assured her. Dragging longing eyes from a sliver of stark chestnut silk, Sophie did her best to feel enthusiasm for Tam's final choice, which went to dangerously plunging necklines and skirts of multi-pleated chiffon which floated as the wearer moved.

'Lucky they had our sizes in the same midnight-blue,' said Lucy, over lunch, and grinned at Sophie. 'A touch of the Marilyn Monroe about them somewhere, so we'd better pray for a calm day, and avoid any hot-air vents.'

'Wear matching cycle shorts to be safe,' said Tam with a giggle.

When they were in the taxi on the way home, exhausted but jubilant after a final raid on the store's shoe and cosmetic departments, Sophie's mobile phone rang.

'Where are you, Sophie?' asked Jago.

Struck dumb for a moment, Sophie pulled herself together with effort. 'In a taxi on the way back to Bayswater, after a ''shop till you drop'' kind of day.'

'I found a flat today,' he said abruptly. 'I'll be moving in shortly. So take down the address. Please,' he added, wrenching out the word in a way which sent Sophie rummaging in her bag for a pen. She wrote the address in her diary, thanked him stiltedly, wished him well in his new home, and, because it was impossible to talk to him while her friends were doing their best to turn deaf ears, rang off.

'Was that the famous Mr X?' asked Tam eagerly. 'I wish I'd met him. Is he gorgeous, Luce?'

'If you like tall, dark and smouldering, yes. What did he want, Sophie?'

'Just to give me his address. He's found a new flat.'

'Aha! He's not going to let you go without a struggle, is he?' gloated Lucy. 'You're weakening, Sophie.'

Which was so near the truth Sophie denied it vehemently and, during the evening, firmly steered the conversation to Tam's wedding and everything to do with it. She contributed her share to it with animation, ate slices of pizza, poured glasses of wine and, on one level, enjoyed the type of occasion rare in the lives of the trio now they were adults. But deep down she yearned to be in her friend's shoes. With Jago in the role of bridegroom.

And Ben to give the bride away?

'Charlotte's doing the flowers, of course,' said Tam. 'I'll take your frocks with me so she's got something to work with.'

'Not girly flowers in our hair, Tam,' implored Lucy.

'I'll give it some thought,' promised the bride, eyeing her friend's expensive crop. 'Not that you could get flowers in that, Luce. Charlotte and Ben are too busy to make it to the wedding by the way,' she told Sophie. 'Two others on the same day, would you believe! Your mother's coming to the important part with Mrs Probert, but they've both passed up the hop in the evening.'

Sophie longed to pass it up too, a feeling which intensified in the weeks that followed when she was back at Highfield. Despite her tan it was obvious to Stephen Laing, and anyone else with half an eye to see, that her holiday had not sent her back to work in the highest of spirits.

She had known beforehand that life would be lonely without Jago when she got back. But she had longed for the trip to Portugal so much she'd convinced herself that afterwards it would be simple to settle back into the routine she'd found perfectly satisfying before meeting Jago. But this was proving impossible. Not least because in her heart of hearts she'd hoped, expected, even, that Jago would get in touch at some point, since he'd taken the trouble to give her his address. But he never did.

Sophie filled her time as best she could, chatted with her mother on the phone rather more than usual, attended her aerobics classes doggedly, went to the cinema in Cheltenham occasionally with Joanna Trenchard, and to the Rose and Crown with Jon Barlow. At weekends she worked long and hard in the garden, spent Saturday nights alone, and accepted gratefully when asked to Sunday lunch again with the Laings.

Weekdays were no problem. At this time of year they were unfailingly hectic, and Sophie was glad of it, happy to work late when problems cropped up with any of the parties or wedding receptions which increased in number at Highfield during the Christmas season.

'I don't mind a bit,' she assured Stephen every time. 'You go home to Anna. I can deal with this.'

Sophie got back to Ivy Lodge late one evening, to find a message waiting from a very angry Glen Taylor.

'You needn't have paid a solicitor to write me a letter, Sophie. I got your message loud and clear last time. I wouldn't set foot in your place again if you begged me on bended knees.'

Sophie's eyes lit up as the message cut off. So Jago hadn't forgotten. In which case she owed him money, since she doubted very much he'd asked his brother to write a solicitor's letter for free.

Glad of the excuse to contact Jago, before she even took her coat off Sophie took out her diary and dialled his mobile number.

'Langham Smith,' came the curt response, and she took in a deep, silent breath to steady herself.

'Sophie here,' she said, after a pause. 'Sophie Marlow.' Just in case he was in any doubt.

'Yes?'

No hello, or enquiry after her health. His tone damped Sophie down like a cold sponge.

'I've had a message from Glen Taylor,' she said, after a pause to recover. 'He's received a solicitor's letter, so I assume you instructed your brother to send it.'

'I did. Why? Is there a problem?'

'Only with payment. How much do I owe your brother?'

'Nothing. I paid him myself.'

'Then I owe *you*—'

'You owe me nothing, Sophie.'

His tone was so final she thanked him formally, put the phone down, and burst into tears.

After working late every night of the week beforehand to make up, Sophie left early for Wales the following Friday afternoon to be in good time for the wedding rehearsal.

'Take photographs, Anna commanded,' said Stephen, as she left.

'I'll try. See you Monday.'

Sophie arrived home for a quick snack with her mother, and decided to walk over to the church. 'Lucy should be there before me. She had the day off.'

Faith Marlow eyed her daughter's pale, tired face with worried eyes. 'Why didn't you do that?'

'I hadn't the heart to ask after my week's holiday.'

'Lucy obviously did.'

Careful, thought Sophie. 'Must dash, Mother—I'll admire your hat when I get back.'

'Your dress is gorgeous, by the way,' said Faith. 'Tam brought it over to Charlotte when they were choosing the flowers. It's hanging in your room.'

'Pleats and chiffon aren't really my cup of tea, Lucy's either,' said Sophie ruefully, 'but Tam was thrilled, so that's all that matters. See you later.'

The rehearsal went off as smoothly as anything ever did in Tam's vicinity, with much hilarity because one of her brothers stood in for the bridegroom forbidden to attend to rule out bad luck. When the session was over Sophie went back to the Hayford home with Lucy for a glass of champagne and a chat with Tam's three brothers, two wives and the four sons two of the brothers had produced.

'Not a granddaughter among them,' said Grenville Hayford, wincing at the noise.

'Which cut the cost on bridesmaid dresses,' his daughter pointed out.

'By Jove, yes,' he said thankfully, and patted her cheek. 'So now you can have a shot at providing me with a granddaughter, my pet.'

'Give me a chance, Daddy!'

'Where are you going on your honeymoon?' asked Lucy.

'No idea.' Tam smiled radiantly. 'David's surprising me. Clothes for the sun, and clothes for the rain, and if I need anything else he'll take me shopping,' she added, unperturbed by catcalls from her brothers.

'He'll rue the day he said that,' said Jasper Hayford, the happily unmarried brother. 'Though to be fair, Tam, you're more interested in horses than clothes. Unlike my beautiful sisters-in-law,' he added, with a mocking bow in their direction.

There was much unoffended laughter from the ladies in question and, after a pleasant interval of light-hearted flirting with Jasper, Sophie caught Lucy's eye and said goodbye to Tam, promising to be at the house bright and early in the morning.

'Just give me time to wash my hair and I'll be with you,' she promised. 'Is someone coming to do yours?'

'Good heavens, no,' said Tam cheerfully. 'I'll do it myself, as usual.'

'Tam never changes, does she?' said Lucy, as she dropped Sophie off. 'Thank God she found someone like David Barclay. Though I wouldn't fancy Mrs Barclay for a mother-in-law myself.'

'You look exhausted, Sophie, so go to bed straight after supper,' said Faith later. 'I asked Ben and Charlotte to eat with us tonight, but they need an early start in the morning, to get flowers finished and delivered for the three weddings. They're coming to lunch on Sunday instead.'

'Why so many weddings? Is there something special about the date tomorrow?'

'No. It just happens that way sometimes. Which is good business, so let's not complain.'

'If anyone's complaining I imagine it's Charlotte!'

Faith smiled. 'That'll be the day.' She hesitated, as though about to say something, then changed her mind and began serving their meal.

Sophie woke early next morning, and leapt out of bed to peer from the window, thankful to find that for once the weather forecast had been accurate and the day was fine. She made a face at the drift of indigo chiffon hanging from the wardrobe door, then tiptoed to the kitchen in her dressing gown to make breakfast for her mother, but found Faith Marlow already at the breakfast table, dressed in serviceable trousers and sweater.

'Good morning, darling, you're early,' she said with a smile, and filled a beaker with tea.

Sophie stared at her in surprise. 'So are you!'

'I can't make it to the wedding after all,' said Faith with regret. 'Charlotte's poorly, so I'm taking over for her.'

'What's wrong?' demanded Sophie in alarm.

'Nothing wrong, darling.' Her mother smiled jubilantly. 'Charlotte's pregnant at last, that's all. She wanted to tell you herself, but in the circumstances I was given permission to break the news first. She's plagued with virulent sickness some mornings, and this is one of them. By this afternoon she'll probably be fine, but for the moment Ben's keeping her in bed.'

'That's wonderful!' Sophie blinked hard. 'I'm so happy for them.'

'Nothing to cry about, pet,' said Faith gently. 'You still look tired. You're obviously working too hard—and your holiday doesn't seem to have done you much good.'

'Busy time since I got back,' said Sophie firmly, and blew her nose. 'Good thing you're so artistic with bridal bouquets, and so on.'

'It was always the side of the business I liked most. But where Tam's concerned Charlotte did the church and delivered the table decorations yesterday, and Ben's on his way as we speak with the rest of her flowers. Tam's wearing some kind of heirloom in those blonde curls of hers, sensible girl.' Mrs Marlow sighed. 'Such a pity I can't be there. Apologise for me to Tam and her father, and beg one of the official photographs.'

'I'm sorry you can't come, Mother. Shame about the hat, too,' said Sophie, getting up to make toast.

'I'll keep it for some other wedding—yours, maybe,' said her mother with a chuckle, and looked at the clock. 'Must dash. Have a good time, give Tam my love, and take a key. I'll work until we close today, to make sure Charlotte toes the line.' Faith smiled. 'If Ben had his way he'd take someone else on in her place and wrap her in cotton wool until the baby arrives.'

Sophie laughed. 'I can just see Charlotte standing for that!' She kissed her mother swiftly. 'Off you go. And give the parents-to-be my congratulations. I'll see them tomorrow.'

After a look in the mirror Sophie had to agree with her mother. She looked tired, her hair was lank, and something drastic had to be done to transform herself into the bridesmaid Tam deserved.

Sophie washed and conditioned her hair to within an inch of its life, and, after a long soak in the bath, with slices of cucumber on her eyes and some expensive green mud on her skin, she viewed the glowing result later with more optimism. By the time Lucy arrived Sophie had twisted her hair into a gleaming, intricate coil, with a few artistic tendrils left loose for once, and decided she might do Tam justice after all.

'Great hair, but what about your face?' demanded Lucy, perfect to the last eyelash.

'It's hours yet to the wedding. I thought I'd leave it until we get to Tam's.'

Sophie made a pot of coffee, and sat down with Lucy at the kitchen table to drink it at leisure. 'Half an hour before we need join the fray.'

Lucy stared down into her cup for a moment, then heaved a sigh and looked up, her eyes heavy with guilt. 'It's no use—I must get it off my chest. I've got something to confess.'

Sophie stared. 'To *me*?'

Lucy nodded. 'I should have told you this before. Paul's coming to the wedding.'

'That's nice. How come?'

'Because—well—Paul and I are together these days,' said Lucy in a rush, and eyed her friend with uncharacteristic awkwardness. 'We tried to tell you last week, but you were in such a state after Mr X left neither of us could bring ourselves to do it.'

'Why ever not, you muggins? I think that's just marvellous, Luce.' Sophie grinned. 'In fact, I was looking at you two that night, thinking what a great pair you made. My infallible intuition, obviously.'

Lucy sagged in relief. 'Then you don't mind? Honestly?'

'Of course I don't mind! Is Paul coming to the church?'

'No, just to the dance. He's driving down later.' Lucy stretched out a hand to touch Sophie's. 'Are you all right, love?'

'About Paul? Of course I am.'

'I meant Mr X.'

Sophie smiled crookedly. 'No, Luce. Not yet. But no more on that subject. This is Tam's day.'

The Hayford household was in uproar when they arrived. The father of the bride had mislaid his favourite cufflinks, Lydia Hayford was rushing round with a seating plan and placecards for the tables arranged round the hall for the wedding breakfast, Prue Hayford was dealing with the caterers, and their respective husbands were out playing football in the garden with their sons to keep them out of the way.

'Jasper,' said Lydia with envy, 'cleared off to the pub to meet some of the guests, lucky blighter. And I couldn't get on with this before because Tam only finished juggling with the place names this morning.'

'Where is Tam?' asked Sophie.

'You won't believe this,' said Prue, coming to join them. 'She's gone for a ride.'

'Oh, we believe it,' said Lucy, grinning. 'Give us a minute to take our finery upstairs, then we'll give you a hand.'

Half an hour later the cufflinks were found, Lucy had sorted out the remaining placecards, Sophie was overseeing the caterers, and Lydia and Prue had been sent upstairs to dress. And with just two hours to go the bride rushed in, beaming, to hug her friends and apologise for being late, explaining she'd just had to give Centaur a gallop on such a lovely day.

'I'll just tell Daddy I'm back, then I'll wash my hair,' she said blithely.

Her bridesmaids exchanged a resigned look. 'I'll do that for you while Sophie does her face,' said Lucy firmly. 'I'm a whizz with a hairdryer.'

'You're a whizz with everything,' said Tam in admiration, and rushed up the staircase, shouting for her father.

Half an hour before they were due to leave for the church Lucy put the finishing touches to the bride's top-knot of blonde curls and carefully placed a small pearl and gold coronet in front of it to hold the short veil back, then allowed Tam to look in the mirror.

'Gosh,' said the bride in awe. 'Is that me?'

'Oh, yes,' said Sophie softly. 'That's you all right, Tam.'

'We go down first, Tam,' said Lucy, blowing a kiss to her friend. 'You wait for a bit, pick up your bouquet, then you come down too. Everyone must surely be ready by this time.'

'Hang on, I haven't given you your flowers,' said Tam. 'Lucy, look in the cupboard over the washbasin. They're in there, keeping cool.'

Lucy opened the cupboard, and whistled her approval. 'Tam, how gorgeous.'

'I asked for something sophisticated, Luce,' said Tam, smiling. 'So Charlotte suggested orchids. She's attached them to velvet covered clips you sort of stick down your dresses at cleavage point.'

Sophie slid the cluster of small, creamy orchids into the hollow between her breasts, and smiled at Tam. 'If I hug you I'll spoil all Luce's good work, but thanks, love. A wonderful idea.' She cocked an eye at Lucy. 'Not even you can object to wearing flowers this way!'

'I would have stuck them in my hair somehow if necessary,' protested Lucy, 'but this is perfect. Thanks, Tam. Come on, let's go.'

The two bridesmaids went swiftly down the stairs together to join the family gathered below, to receive glasses of champagne from Jasper Hayford, now back in the bosom of his family.

'You look delicious, girls,' he said, with a leer. 'Where's Tam?'

'Coming any minute,' whispered Lucy.

'Everyone ready?' he demanded, and received murmurs of ascent just as Tam appeared at the top of the stairs.

'To the bride,' said everyone in unison, and raised their glasses in toast as Tamsin Hayford sailed down the stairs in all her smiling gold and white glory.

The wedding party walked in procession to the church, which was close by, fortunately for the bridesmaids, whose spike-heeled sandals had never been intended for hiking. They followed after the bride and her proud father, with the rest of the family bringing up the rear, and a large proportion of the village population lining the route to wish the bride well.

'Thank heavens it isn't blowing a gale, or raining, or both,' muttered Sophie, smiling on all sides as they kept hold of Tam's train by the loops provided for the purpose.

The wedding day was not only fine, but crisp and cloudless, with autumnal sunshine that turned Tam's hair into a gilt aureole as they waited in the porch while the ushers and the rest of the family took their seats. The organist checked her mirror, paused, then with verve began to play 'The Entry of the Queen of Sheba'.

Tam turned to grin at her friends. 'Daddy's choice.'

The bridesmaids let the bridal train rustle to the floor, and with a last smile at them over her shoulder Tamsin Hayford went forward on her father's arm to meet her bridegroom.

Sophie received Tam's bouquet at the altar, Lucy held the hymn book for them to share, both of them touched when they saw that the first hymn was 'All Things Bright and Beautiful', sung so often by the three of them at primary school.

After the service, which included a solo from the bride's nephew, transformed from muddy, footballing scruff to cherubic boy soprano, there was much kissing in the vestry, the final hymn was sung, and at last the wedding party progressed down the aisle to the triumphant strains of Wagner. This time Sophie walked on the opposite side of the aisle, smiling at Tam's relatives as she followed the wedding party, but when the group neared the door her heart stopped for an instant, and resumed with a sickening thud. The man standing at the back was not a wild figment of her imagination, as she'd thought for a split second, but Jago Langham Smith in the tall, morning-suited flesh.

CHAPTER NINE

SOPHIE'S eyes met Jago's for a long, startled moment, then slid away. Walk, she told her feet. Smile, she ordered her mouth. And both, amazingly, obeyed. Then she was outside the church, held hostage with the bridal party for the official photographs, with several unofficial photographers dodging about while various groups posed with the bride and her beaming groom, who gazed down at Tam the whole time as though amazed at his good fortune.

'Now the two bridesmaids together,' called the photographer, and Lucy came to stand with Sophie.

'You've spotted Mr X?' muttered Lucy from the corner of her mouth.

'Yes.'

'What's he doing here? Did you know he was coming?'

'No.'

'Oh, boy!'

With Jago watching from the shadow of a yew tree, the photo session seemed endless, until deliverance came at last when Tam threw up a hand, laughing.

'Enough. Let's go home, everyone.'

Jago moved swiftly to intercept Sophie when the bridal pair moved off together, with parents and various relatives following in convoy behind.

'What are you doing here?' she whispered fiercely.

He took a gilt-edged card from his pocket. 'His Honour Grenville Hayford invited me to his daughter's

wedding, of course. Did you think I was a gatecrasher?'
His eyes were hard. 'I had no idea this was the wedding
you meant.'

'Hey, you two, let me introduce you,' said Jasper, as
Lucy, with a worried look at her friend, went off with
the best man. 'Smithy, meet Tam's bosom pal, Miss
Sophie Marlow—a lady I've been privileged to know
since she was a baby.'

Sophie stiffened, hardly able to believe her ears. She
stared incredulously. Jago Langham Smith was actually
the fabled Smithy, Jasper's college friend?

'We've met,' said Jago baldly, and Jasper flushed.

'Oh, my God, yes,' he muttered, comprehension hitting him. 'Of course you have.'

'What a surprise to see you again, Jago,' Sophie said
politely.

Jasper looked from one set face to the other, his eyes
speculative. 'Do I take it you've met each other since—
I mean, lately?'

'By chance, yes. I finished off my latest book at a
friend's place on the estate Sophie manages,' said Jago,
his face like a mask.

'Jasper!' bellowed one of his brothers. 'Put a move
on, will you?'

Jasper Hayford eyed the other two uneasily, but Jago
waved him off.

'Go on. I'll escort Sophie back to the house. You'd
better make a run for it.'

'Small world,' observed Sophie, as they watched
Jasper race to join his family.

'If I'd known I wouldn't have come,' Jago assured
her starkly as they began the walk back to Hayford
House.

'But since you are here we'll just behave like adults

and make the best of it,' Sophie said briskly. 'In fact,' she added, 'now I realise who you are in relation to the Hayfords, it's amazing we've never run into each other before.'

'I suppose it is.' Jago shrugged. 'I used to come here with Jasper quite a bit when we were younger, even after we were both called to the bar. But we operate in different parts of the country these days.'

'It's quite a shock to discover you're the famous Smithy,' she said, still trying to take it in.

'Famous?'

'Absolutely. Lucy and I had crushes on rock stars, and so on, but the object of Tam's teenage passion was her brother's gorgeous friend. You bet you were famous,' said Sophie.

'I did nothing at all to encourage Tam,' said Jago stiffly.

'You didn't have to—smile! We're on camera.'

The photographer was waiting to take shots of the guests as they entered the house. Sophie smiled radiantly into his lens, and linked her arm through Jago's, feeling it tense like an iron bar under her hand. Inside the house Tam was standing with her new husband at the foot of the stairs, kissing everyone as they arrived. Her eyes lit up when she saw Jago.

'Smithy! I get my kiss at last.' She fluttered her eyelashes at her new husband. 'I used to lie awake dreaming about this at one time, David.'

'You're incorrigible, Mrs Barclay,' said Jago, then kissed her on both cheeks and shook hands with the grinning bridegroom to congratulate him.

'You've met Smithy at last, then?' said Tam, hugging Sophie. 'He was supposed to bring some woman, but they've split up recently. I've sorted the place cards so you sit next to each other, so do comfort the poor lamb.'

'Of course I will,' Sophie promised, and turned to the poor lamb with a smile which won her a sardonic lift of eyebrow. 'First we say polite nothings to Tam's in-laws, then we talk to the Judge,' she informed him as he took two glasses of champagne from a waiter. 'After that we separate and circulate.'

'You were told to comfort me,' he reminded her.

'You look in precious little need of comfort to me.'

'You're wrong there—' Jago broke off as they reached the bridegroom's parents, obliged to join Sophie in saying the right things before they could go on to greet the bride's father. 'How do you do, sir?'

'Smithy!' Judge Grenville Hayford's face creased in a welcoming smile as he shook Jago's hand. 'Good to see you, my boy. You've been neglecting us.' He put out an arm and drew Sophie close. 'But I can see you're in delightfully good hands. Look after this rascal, sweetheart. Some female's had the bad taste to jilt him, I hear.'

'How true,' murmured Jago, and shot a narrowed, gleaming glance at Sophie before embarking on the kind of legal shop talk much loved by the Judge, giving her the opportunity to excuse herself to find Lucy.

'Back in a minute,' Lucy told Bruce, the best man, and hurried upstairs to Tam's room with Sophie. 'How are you coping?' she demanded.

'Quite well, really. Once I'd recovered from the shock.'

'Coming face to face with Mr X?'

'That was just for openers,' said Sophie. 'My Mr X has yet another alias up his sleeve.' She paused dramatically. 'He also happens to be Jasper's old buddy, the object of Tam's teenage lust.' Sophie turned away to make repairs to her face. 'His full name is Jago Langham Smith, aka Smithy, the man Tam was nuts about for years.'

Her friend goggled. 'You're kidding!'

'I'm not. Tam's famous Smithy he is, only somehow we never actually met him in the flesh.'

'You have now!' said Lucy drily.

'I have indeed.' Sophie rearranged a stray lock of hair, then smiled philosophically at her friend. 'Come on, bridesmaid. Let's get back to the job.'

Sophie wasn't sure if she felt sorry, or in some ways wildly happy, to be sitting next to Jago at a table where Lucy and the best man, plus Jasper Hayford and one of his young girl cousins, made up the number. Champagne and badinage flowed as the caterers served the meal, but Sophie kept to the mineral water Jago requested for her, and saved a solitary glass of wine for the toasts.

'Thank you,' she whispered, then looked up to smile across the table in reassurance when she found Jasper Hayford's worried blue eyes on them.

And after the speeches were over and the cake cut and handed out, the bride and groom circulated among the guests to talk with everyone, and the first half of the day was virtually over.

Lucy went to join her mother, the best man left to joke with the bride and groom, and Jasper, after a significant look at Jago, swept his cousin off to chat with other relatives, leaving his friend alone with Sophie at the table.

'Sophie,' said Jago in an undertone, 'I need to talk to you.'

'Talk away.'

'Can't we go somewhere else?'

'Certainly not.'

His jaw clenched. 'I just wanted you to know I'm putting up at the Red Lion. If you prefer I can easily stay put there this evening rather than spoil things for you.'

Sophie turned a scornful look on him. 'If you didn't turn up at the dance the Hayfords would want to know why. And you would spoil things for Tam, not me.'

'You're right, of course.' His mouth twisted. 'I haven't been able to think straight since I saw you walk down the aisle behind Tam. So what happens now?'

'Everyone separates for a breather, to recharge batteries for tonight.'

'Sorry to intrude,' said Lucy, coming back to join them. 'Want a lift home, Sophie, or are you staying on here?' she added, as Jago stood up.

'I'll come with you,' said Sophie promptly. 'We'll see you later, Jago.'

'I'll look forward to it,' he assured her, then smiled wryly at Lucy. 'An unexpected pleasure to meet you again, Miss Probert.'

'Unexpected all round—and do make it Lucy.' Her eyes gleamed. 'One way and another I feel I know you well enough.'

'She means because Tam used to rattle on so much about you,' said Sophie hastily, her cheeks hot as she met the gleam in Jago's eyes.

'I'll see you later, Sophie,' he said with emphasis, and gave her the smile last seen before the storm clouds gathered on the morning of their departure from Quinta Viana.

'Wow, what a smile! Does it mean you're on a promise?' muttered Lucy, as they went to take temporary leave of the bride.

'More like a threat.' Sophie shivered. 'Thank heavens Mother couldn't make it to the wedding.'

'Gosh, yes.' Lucy looked at her anxiously. 'Are you all right?'

'As well as can be expected!'

'I'll call for you about eight-thirty, then, after Paul arrives,' said Lucy, as they went off to find Mrs Probert.

When Sophie got back to Ty Mawr she found her mother had left a message on the phone.

'Sophie, I'm staying on here for dinner. Charlotte's better now, and insists on feeding me. I hope all went well. See you tomorrow if you're late.'

Sophie kicked off the high-heeled sandals, exchanged her dress for a bathrobe, then made herself some tea, and curled up on her mother's sofa to drink it, glad of the breather before she tackled the rest of the festivities. Though Jago, she thought with a little smile of satisfaction, would find the evening session very different from the small, private wedding breakfast. Tam was sure to have invited all the friends of their youth, which meant no lack of dancing partners for her bridesmaids. Then she shivered suddenly, deeply grateful to Charlotte for keeping her mother-in-law from the wedding. Faith Marlow had been so bitter about Ben's lawyer at the time it was unlikely she'd feel any warmer towards him now. Even less so if she discovered her daughter had fallen in love with him.

By the time Paul and Lucy arrived to pick her up Sophie had revived herself with a quick shower, redone her face, and brushed her hair free from the coil to fall to the shoulders of the fluttering, diaphanous dress so foreign to her own taste.

'You've taken your hair down—good,' said Lucy, when Sophie slid into Paul's car.

'Hi, Paul.' Sophie smiled at him reassuringly. 'Terrific news.'

'Thanks, love,' he said with relief. 'I would have told you ages ago, but Luce kept dragging her feet.'

'Blessings on you both, my children,' she said firmly.

'I've told Paul your mystery man was at the wedding,' said Lucy.

'Bit of a facer,' he commented, meeting Sophie's eyes in the driving mirror.

'Especially when it turns out he's an old friend of Jasper Hayford!'

When they arrived at the church hall, which Charlotte and her helpers had transformed with greenery and flowers the day before, the small band was belting out the old standards Tam had requested.

'Hurry up,' said Lucy, as the three of them went in. 'We only just made it before Tam.'

Sophie clapped and cheered with the rest when a drumroll from the band heralded the arrival of the bride and groom, and Tam, minus her veil and the detachable train from her bridal gown, took to the floor with her beaming bridegroom to complete a couple of circuits in correct, school-taught waltz-time before the band swung into something more upbeat.

'Everybody dance!' cried Tam.

Sophie had spotted Jago the moment she arrived. His formal wedding gear exchanged for a lightweight suit she remembered from Portugal, he was at the bar, laughing with Jasper in company with a woman dressed with such expensive simplicity Sophie took an even deeper dislike to her gauzy chiffon, and cursed her impulse to brush her hair loose.

'Sophie!' said a familiar voice, and she turned to find Harry Statham approaching, arms outstretched and a wide grin on his face. In his youth the vicar's son had been a leather-jacketed rebel with long hair and attitude, but now appeared so much the perfect pillar of the establishment Sophie laughed, delighted, as he hugged her.

'What happened to the earrings and flowing locks, Dr Statham?'

'Gone, alas, like my youth, too soon,' he said, giving her a smacking kiss.

'Are those bags under your eyes hard work or debauchery?'

'A bit of both. Where's Luce?'

'Over there, in a fancy frock like mine. Are you married yet?'

He shook his head, grinning. 'Still cutting a swathe through the nursing staff at the Royal.'

Harry pulled Sophie onto the floor to dance with the frenetic energy remembered from the school parties of their teenage years, and she joined in with enthusiasm, hoping Jago was jealously watching.

But Jago was not watching, jealously or otherwise. When Harry took her to the bar for a drink afterwards, Sophie felt murder in her heart when she spotted Jago dancing with the woman she'd seen earlier.

'What will you have?' said Harry.

Hemlock, thought Sophie, and smiled at her old friend. 'Something long, cold and non-alcoholic, please.'

Several more friends came hurrying to join them, and soon Harry and Sophie were catching up on who was doing what and where. Lucy and Paul came to join in, and eventually Sophie danced with every man in turn, including David Barclay and the best man, even with Judge Hayford, who proved to be very light on his feet for such a large, imposing man.

'Having a good time, sweetheart?' he asked, as he guided Sophie through a surprisingly nimble foxtrot.

'Fabulous,' Sophie assured him, and followed his eye to where Tam was dancing with Jasper, her radiance enough to light up the room on its own. 'She's so happy, Judge.'

'I know, and I thank God for it.' He smiled wryly. 'But I'll miss her.'

'She's only moving to the other side of the village,' Sophie comforted him.

'I'll still miss her!' Judge Hayford looked down into her face searchingly. 'No wedding bells for you yet, Sophie?'

'Not me. Married to my job.'

'Damn waste!' He turned sharply as someone tapped him on the shoulder.

'Mind if I cut in?' said Jago, smiling.

'I certainly do mind, Smithy.' Judge Hayford smiled benevolently. 'But because it's you, I'll let her go.'

The band had changed from a foxtrot to something Sophie had trouble in identifying. 'What do you suppose this is?' she asked, to mask her usual respiratory problem when close to Jago.

'A rumba, possibly?' he said into her ear.

'I can't do that.'

'Neither can I. So we just undulate on the spot in time to the music. God, I thought I'd never get you to myself,' he muttered, his hand burning her back through the chiffon.

'You were pretty well occupied yourself,' she retorted.

His eyes gleamed down into hers. 'Jealous?'

'No way.'

'I was! I wanted to drag you away from your playmates by your hair. Which,' he added, his breath scorching her ear, 'I much prefer loose like that. Though I deeply disapprove of your dress.'

Sophie tipped her head back to look at him. 'Why?'

He looked down his nose at her. 'Because you can practically see through the damn thing!'

'Only the top layer,' she protested. 'There's a sort of slip underneath.'

'I know exactly what's underneath,' he muttered, with a look which made her shiver.

When the sensuous rumba changed to a blast of rock and roll Jago took her by the hand and led her from the floor to the far corner of the bar, now deserted while everybody went wild on the floor. 'How did you get here?' he asked abruptly.

'In Paul's car.'

'I'll drive you home.'

'But—'

'No buts, Sophie.' His eyes held hers relentlessly.

She nodded, dry-mouthed, and Jago's hand crushed hers.

'When can we leave?'

'After the bride and groom leave.' Sophie turned with a smile as Jasper came to join them. 'Everything's gone wonderfully well.'

'Amazingly so, when you think Tam organised it,' he said, grinning. 'My father was all for a wedding breakfast in a five-star hotel with a ballroom, but Tam wouldn't hear of it. Did you enjoy your hen-night, by the way?' he added.

'What did you do?' asked Jago, keeping firm hold of Sophie's hand.

'The three of us shared a pizza and a bottle of bubbly

at Lucy's place.' She smiled. 'Tam's choice. Though fully approved by Lucy and me.'

'Other women go abroad for entire weekends or paint the town red, Smithy, but not my little sister,' said Jasper, eyeing their clasped hands.

'Why do you call him that?' asked Sophie.

'When we first roomed together in college Jasper and Jago sounded too much like a comedy turn,' he said, shrugging.

'So I became Smithy.' Jago exchanged a long hard look with his friend.

'Right,' said Jasper hurriedly. 'Must go and do my bit. See you later.'

Sophie turned to Jago when they were alone. 'If you're driving me home—'

'Not if, Sophie. I am.'

'Then once Tam leaves I'd better tell Lucy.'

When the band struck up the wedding march Tam and David began making the rounds of the hall, and Sophie moved from the bar with Jago to be ready when the bride and groom reached them.

Tam enveloped Sophie in a hug, crushing the orchids. 'Though I think they were a bit squashed before then,' she said, laughing, and fluttered her lashes at Jago. 'I saw you smooching with Sophie just now.'

'You're a minx, Tam,' he said with affection, and looked at the bridegroom. 'Take care of her.'

'I will,' said David Barclay with fervour. 'Come on, wife, our carriage awaits.'

All the guests rushed outside, roaring with laughter when the bride and groom climbed into Tam's ancient pick-up, which had been festooned with balloons and tin cans, various messages scrawled on it in toothpaste, and a cluster of rubber boots tied to the tailgate.

'Where on earth are they going in that?' said Jago above the laughter, as the bridegroom crashed the gears before driving down the lane, cans clattering, and everyone cheering under the fairy lights strung across the church hall.

'Just to the other side of the village. David's bought a house near Tam's riding school. They fly off to some mysterious destination tomorrow.'

'Not so mysterious,' murmured Jago, as Lucy and Paul came to join them. 'I'll tell you later.'

'Hey, you two. Aren't you coming back in?' said Lucy. 'The band's going to play for hours yet.'

'Sophie's tired,' said Jago, and exchanged a straight look with Paul. 'Don't worry. I'll drive her home.'

'Right,' said Paul promptly. 'See you tomorrow, then, Sophie. Come on, Luce. Let's party.'

Lucy gave Sophie a quick hug, then looked hard at Jago. 'Look after her.'

'I will.'

'I must say goodnight to the Judge,' insisted Sophie, and because the round of leave-taking took in all the Hayfords half an hour had elapsed before they were finally in Jago's car.

'I thought we'd never get away,' said Jago. 'How far is it to your family's garden centre?'

'My mother doesn't live there now. When Ty Mawr— the local manor house—was converted into flats she bought one of the smallest ones.' Sophie looked up at the familiar profile. 'For obvious reasons I won't be able to ask you in.'

'Even if you had the slightest intention of doing so,' he cut back at her.

After the shock of seeing him at the wedding, coupled with the high-octane emotion of the entire day, Sophie's

own emotions were in such turmoil she wasn't sure what
her intentions were. But one fact emerged from the rest
with total clarity. She wanted—needed—to be in Jago's
arms so badly at this moment nothing else in the world
mattered.

She gave him directions to the old house and, when
they arrived, told Jago to park his car next to hers in the
pool of darkness under the pine trees which shaded the
visitors' car park at Ty Mawr.

'My mother puts her car in the communal garage
round the back,' she told him, when Jago switched off
the lights and killed the engine. 'So I don't know
whether she's in or not.'

'Will she be expecting you?'

'Not until a lot later than this, probably. I took a key.'
Sophie undid the seatbelt and turned towards him.
'Jago,' she said without preamble, 'was it Jasper who
asked you to defend Ben?'

Jago nodded soberly. 'Your mother asked the
Hayfords for help, but because your brother was a friend
none of them could defend him. So Jasper asked me.
And the moment I realised who you were I wished to
God he hadn't.' He shifted in his seat, staring through
the windscreen into the darkness. 'You know, Sophie, I
walked out of your friend's flat that day, determined to
forget I'd ever met you.'

'I rather gathered that. But I waited, hoping you'd
look back.'

Jago turned to look at her. 'You know what would
have happened if I had.'

'What?' she whispered.

'This,' he said, and then she was in his arms, where
she'd longed to be, and Jago kissed her until neither of
them could breathe, then held her as close as he could

in the confined space. 'It's a long time since I made love in a car,' he said into her hair.

'Me too.'

'Who with?' he demanded, tipping her face up to his.

'Harry Statham, the vicar's son. The man I danced most with tonight. He drove me home in his father's car from our last school party.' Sophie trailed a finger down Jago's cheek. 'But we got in the back seat.'

'Did you now?'

'Just kisses, of course.'

Jago slid a hand beneath the fragile chiffon to touch the heart beating there for him. 'Nothing like this?'

'There's never been anything like this,' she said in a stifled voice, and reached up to bring his head down to hers.

There was silence for a long timeless interval, and at last Jago raised his head and released Sophie to take her face in shaking hands. 'This is agony,' he panted. 'I don't want to make love to you in a car, I want you in my arms, in my bed, in my *life*.'

A statement which simplified everything for Sophie. Now she was here in Jago's arms again she couldn't understand why she'd been so adamant on the subject before.

'Good. Because I've changed my mind,' she told him.

Jago dropped his hands and moved away a little. 'About what, exactly?' he demanded, in a tone more suitable to the courtroom.

'About us. I've tried to get used to life without you,' she said unsteadily. 'But I just can't do it.'

Jago got out and came round the car to help her from it. He drew her into his arms and held her close, his cheek against her hair. 'I can't, either, darling. Even if we hadn't met again today, I would have come after you to Highfield. All that high-flown talk about not being able to beg was just pride.' He gave an exultant laugh. 'But some deep-dyed chauvinistic streak of mine can't help feeling triumphant that you weakened first.'

'Is that what I've done?'

'Of course you have,' he said, with such smug arrogance she chuckled, and leaned against him when he pulled her closer. 'You're mine, Sophie Marlow, and you know it.'

'Yes,' she said, beyond even trying to deny it.

'Say it, then.'

'I'm yours,' she muttered into his chest, and he crushed her close.

'So,' said Jago, suddenly brisk. 'Since I'm here on the spot there's no time like the present. Not tonight, of course. But certainly tomorrow, before we leave.'

Sophie pulled away in alarm. 'What do you mean?'

'It's the perfect time to introduce me to your family, so I can tell them I want to marry you—'

'*Marry* me?' she said blankly.

'Of course. What did you think we were talking about? And because this is the first and only time I've ever proposed marriage to anyone, Miss Marlow,' he said reprovingly, 'a little more enthusiasm wouldn't go amiss.'

'But I had no idea—' Sophie turned away in shock.

Jago was ominously silent for a while. 'So what did you mean about changing your mind?' he asked at last.

She turned to face him. 'I meant seeing each other when we could—occasional weekends together. I can't *marry* you, Jago.'

He stood with arms folded and legs slightly apart, looking down his nose in the way she knew so well. 'I see,' he said at last. 'Whereas for a wild moment I thought you'd actually agreed to be legally mine, to cleave only unto me, no matter what your family thought of the idea.'

She reached out a hand in appeal. 'I don't have to marry you to belong to you, Jago!'

'I disagree. So I'm declining your kind offer. I refuse to lurk in the shadows of your life, like a dirty secret. Husband, lover, partner, whatever you like. I demand official status of some kind, Sophie.' He seized her by the shoulders. 'So for God's sake let's bring it out in the open.'

'No,' she said flatly, and felt cold when his hands fell away.

Jago surveyed her in silence for a while, something about his attitude, even in the darkness, conveying his bitterness to Sophie. 'We seem to have played this scene before,' he said at last, and to her consternation opened the car door.

'Where are you going?' she said in dismay.

'Back where I belong.' He shrugged negligently. 'It's goodbye again, Sophie Marlow. And this time for good.'

'Goodbye?' she repeated blankly, unable to believe this was happening.

'By the way,' said Jago casually, 'I know where Tam's going for her honeymoon.'

'Oh?' At this moment in time, fond though she was of Tam, Sophie had no attention to spare for her.

'Jasper Hayford was the friend who organised the Quinta Viana for the little holiday you and I spent together,' said Jago tonelessly. 'At the same time, he informs me, he secured it as his present to his little sister for her honeymoon.'

Sophie breathed in shakily. 'Quite a surprise.'

'Isn't it!' Jago's teeth showed white for a moment in

a tigerish smile. 'Hilarious, really. You know, I actually had some cockeyed, romantic idea of taking you back there as *my* bride one day, Sophie.' His voice hardened. 'But something tells me our little idyll was all the honeymoon I'm going to get.'

CHAPTER TEN

'YOU weren't very late coming home,' said Faith Marlow over breakfast next morning. 'But I was half asleep, so I didn't rush out to ask how it all went.'

Sophie launched into an animated account of the wedding reception, careful to avoid mention of Jago. 'The dance was great fun. Lots of people I knew, including Harry Statham, so I didn't lack for partners.' She got up. 'By the mouthwatering smell coming from the oven the roast is in, so hand over the vegetables and I'll get started.'

'I can do that if you're tired.'

'No way. You were the one working yesterday.'

'Did Harry bring you home last night?' asked Faith.

'No.' Sophie paid close attention to the potato she was peeling. 'Luce wanted to stay on so a friend of Jasper's volunteered. Carrots next?'

The lunch was a happy affair, with Ben proud as punch and very protective of his wife, and Charlotte so full of joy about her baby that late that afternoon, after a swift visit to the Probert house to report to an anxious Lucy, Sophie drove back to Highfield feeling more justified than ever in keeping Jago away from her family. But the self-righteous glow soon faded. Jago wanted her for his wife. And he was the only man on the planet she wanted for a husband. But to achieve that she would be forced to cut herself off from her family. Which brought her back, desolate, to square one.

There was no message from Jago when Sophie got

back to Ivy Lodge, but she leapt to her feet expectantly when the phone rang later.

'It's only me,' said Lucy. 'We just got back. Are you all right?'

'Just dandy.'

'Bad as that! I couldn't ask in front of Mother, so tell me what happened last night.'

'Jago proposed. I refused.'

There was a long pause.

'Say that again?' demanded Lucy.

'You heard me. And before you start about gathering rosebuds and so on, I did offer an alternative of weekends of illicit passion together whenever possible. But I was turned down flat.'

'*What?* The man's an idiot! So what happens now?'

'Nothing.' Sophie managed a laugh. 'What really eats me, Luce, is that each time we part—with monotonous regularity—I stand there like a dummy while Jago comes up with a really great exit line. Which reminds me. I know where Tam's going on honeymoon.'

'How?'

'Jago took great pleasure in telling me that the happy pair are probably sitting on the veranda of the Quinta Viana as we speak.'

'What?' Lucy whistled. 'He really wanted to hurt you.'

'He did.'

'As much as you hurt him, maybe?'

'Whose side are you on, Lucy Probert?'

'Yours. But think about it. Even on short acquaintance, Jago doesn't seem the type to hand out marriage proposals very often—'

'He said mine was the first,' said Sophie despondently.

'And you turned him down. The first proposal he's ever made, even though he's successful careerwise, no turn-off in the looks department, and must have had women lusting after him from puberty. '

'Lucy!'

'The point I'm making, dearest, is that you've dealt the man a body blow. So don't be surprised if he looks round for someone to kiss it better.'

It was a thought which tormented Sophie through the following week, to the point that by the weekend, after losing a pitched battle with herself, she rang Jago's new flat, and stood, tense, as she waited for him to pick up.

'Isobel Kidd,' said a crisp voice, followed by a stifled laugh. 'Sorry, sorry, this is Jago Langham Smith's—'

Sophie put the phone down, passionately grateful she'd had the forethought to withhold her number. Lucy was right. Jago had been quick to find balm for his wounded ego. And it hurt far more, because he'd gone back to Isobel for it, than if he'd found someone new.

The period before Christmas was always a hectic time at Highfield, with parties and wedding receptions every week in addition to the conferences that were the venue's bread and butter. Sophie was fiercely glad to be run off her feet, put in extra time at weekends, and arrived back at Ivy Lodge as late as she could every night. Her mother, she learned from their telephone exchanges, was equally busy at the garden centre, putting up garlands and holly, decking out Santa's grotto, and helping out with the sale of Christmas trees, and the poinsettia plants much in demand as gifts for elderly female relatives.

'I hope you get paid overtime,' teased Sophie.

'No amount of overtime can repay the debt I owe Ben!'

Which, Sophie thought in despair, said it all.

Shortly before Christmas Stephen asked Sophie to do him a big favour.

'Anything I can, boss,' she assured him.

'Anna's getting worried about her Christmas shopping. How would you fancy taking a day off tomorrow and driving my wife to Cheltenham?'

Sophie beamed at him. 'I'd just love to!'

Stephen sighed with relief. 'Fantastic. I loathe shopping. Anna can have a peaceful browse with you, treat you to lunch, and pick up the girls from the Traceys' on the way home.'

Anna Laing was like a child let out of school when Sophie went to pick her up next day. 'This is such fun,' she said, settling into the car. 'Stephen has kittens if I drive myself any distance these days, and, as you well know, he insists on chauffering me to the antenatal clinic at St Catherine's every time.'

'Good thing, too. Ben's just the same about Charlotte already—I just hope he lasts out the course!'

They chuckled together and, because the day was fine for once, enjoyed their shopping spree enormously. Sophie carried all the parcels, made sure they stopped for coffee and lunch, and the moment Anna began to flag insisted they go home.

'I promised Stephen I'd look after you,' she said firmly. 'So you wait here, and I'll jog over to the car park and bring the car round.'

When the parcels were packed into the car, Anna sighed wearily as she fastened her seatbelt. 'That's it. *Finito*. Everything else comes from the village shop.'

'How do you feel?'

'Whacked, but triumphant now I've got the girls' presents. Thanks a million, Sophie—I was getting a bit uptight about it all.'

'Are you having your families as usual?'

'Just overnight on Christmas Day, not the usual week. Stephen put his foot down.' Anna shifted a little in her seat. 'How about you, Sophie? Off home?'

'Yes. Stephen's given me the week off.'

Anna gave her a wry, sidelong smile. 'You look, forgive me for mentioning it, as if you could do with it.'

'I know that,' said Sophie ruefully. 'I saw myself in a mirror while you were buying miracle face cream for your mother. I would have bought some too, only—'

'It's not skin cream you need,' said Anna, nodding. 'But I won't pester you for details—ouch!' She breathed in sharply.

'What is it?' asked Sophie in alarm. 'Indigestion?'

'God, I hope so!'

Sophie gulped. 'How far along are you?'

'Six months,' said Anna through her teeth, and winced again. She shot Sophie an apologetic look. 'Perhaps a call in at St Catherine's might be an idea.'

'*Right.*' Desperate to put her foot down, Sophie somehow fought the urge to break the speed limit on the way to the hospital. When they arrived Anna was put in a wheelchair and taken off at once to await a consultant, and Sophie went outside into the car park to ring Stephen.

'Dear God!' he said hoarsely. 'Tell Anna I'll be there as soon as I can.'

While she was outside Sophie rang Nina Tracey, who assured her that the twins could sleep over if necessary.

'Thanks a lot, Nina,' said Sophie with relief. 'Give them my love. I'll get back in touch as soon as I can.'

Anna was given a scan which confirmed that all was well with the baby, despite the cramps which had frightened her out of her wits. She'd been put to bed, and Sophie was sitting with her, receiving instructions, when Stephen came in, wild-eyed and frantic. Sophie quietly removed herself to go outside and ring Nina Tracey to report that Anna was fine, but was being kept in overnight to make sure.

'How are the twins?' she added.

'Anxious. We've seen to Dino, they've had supper, but they're not terribly keen on staying the night. Normally they adore sleepovers, but this is different.'

'If Stephen wants to hang on here, I can pick them up,' offered Sophie.

Sophie drove back to Long Ashley, collected Robyn and Daisy, and serenely allayed their fears about their mother while she drove them home. After she'd supervised baths and bedtime Stephen put in an appearance, looking as haggard as Sophie felt. She made him an omelette when he returned from checking on his little girls, sat down with him at the kitchen table to make sure he ate it, and put a slug of brandy in the coffee she made him afterwards.

'Thanks. You're a godsend, Sophie,' he sighed, and eyed her ruefully. 'You must be shattered.'

'I am.' She shuddered. 'When Anna felt pains in the car I almost died of fright.'

'I'll make damned sure she takes it easy from now on,' he said emphatically, and cast a bloodshot eye at Sophie. 'She's been overdoing it. It's the same every Christmas, but this year that's it. Enough's enough.'

'I must go,' said Sophie, yawning. 'If the girls are safely asleep let's take Anna's shopping from my boot.'

When Sophie got home a stack of Christmas cards

was waiting for her. She chuckled over messages from old friends, then caught her breath when she found one of the envelopes contained only photographs. She blinked back tears as she gazed at the Quinta Viana, gilded in morning sunshine, at herself laughing under a palm tree in the garden, another of Jago, smiling at her with a look in his eye which made it plain he meant to seize her in his arms the instant she'd taken the shot. In the final picture they were together, the photograph taken by the waiter at one of the cafés where they'd lunched in the sun.

Sophie scrabbled round in the envelope, but there was no note. Her first reaction was a telephone call to Jago to thank him. But the prospect of getting Isobel again changed her mind. Instead she took one of the formal Highfield Christmas cards from the pile she was about to send off, scribbled her thanks on one of them for the photographs, and addressed it to Jago's new flat. Then she frowned, her eye caught by the envelope with the photographs. There was no stamp. It had been delivered by hand!

Sophie flew out of the house and down the path, but there was no car anywhere in sight, other than her own. And no lights on in the Frasers' cottage. She trudged back into the house in dejection, furious with a fate which had arranged for her to be out the one and only time Jago came to see her.

Sophie was on her way upstairs to bed when the doorbell rang. She looked at her watch, pulse racing. Just after eleven. She went back down very slowly, expectation building so fiercely inside her she was as taut as a drawn bow when she reached the door.

'Who is it?' she called.

'Jago.'

Sophie stood motionless for a moment, then she slid back the bolt, took off the safety chain and unlocked the door. Jago Langham Smith stood looking down at her, formal in black tie and dinner jacket, his face haggard and unsmiling. And everything in the world she'd ever wanted.

'Hello, Sophie,' he said quietly.

'Hello.'

His eyes dropped to her bare feet, and Sophie moved back, heart thumping.

'Come in.'

'Won't I be keeping you up?'

'It's not that late.' She went into the sitting room to turn on the lamps she'd just switched off. 'Can I offer you a drink, or coffee?' she asked politely, as he followed her.

'Nothing, thanks. I've been dining up at Highfield.'

'Here at Highfield?' she repeated blankly.

'A friend invited me to the legal dinner here tonight. You must have known about it?'

'Oh. Yes.' But she'd assumed it was for legal eagles of the local variety.

'When Joanna told me you hadn't been in today, I called round earlier to see if you were ill, but no luck.' He paused, his eyes moving over her face. 'You look very pale, Sophie. *Are* you ill?'

'No, just tired.' Sophie described the trauma which had crowned the day's shopping. 'Afterwards I stayed at End House to make Stephen Laing an omelette—'

'You're good at those.'

Their eyes met.

'The photographs are lovely,' she said, looking away. 'I've written to thank you.'

'Couldn't you have rung me?'

Sophie's chin flew up. 'No.'

'Why not?'

Her eyes flashed. 'You know why not!'

'Afraid I might have mistaken a call for a change of heart?' he demanded harshly.

'You're the one with the change of heart,' she threw at him. 'And a pretty swift one at that.'

Jago's eyes narrowed. 'What the hell are you talking about?'

'*Who*, not what. Miss Isobel Kidd, to be specific. The lady who answered the phone when I was stupid enough to ring you one night.'

To Sophie's fury Jago relaxed suddenly, his eyes bright with amusement. 'Ah. I see.'

'I'm glad you find it so funny,' she snapped.

He shrugged. 'Isobel called in that evening with some mail for me. I gave her a drink. We talked shop. I called a taxi. She went home.'

'None of which is anything to do with me,' said Sophie loftily, and glanced at her watch. 'It's a long drive back for you, and it's late—'

'I'm staying at the Rose and Crown.' Jago gave her the sudden, heart-stopping smile she could never resist. 'So if the offer of coffee still holds good I'd be happy to accept.'

Sophie turned on her bare heel and marched along the hall to the kitchen, with Jago close behind. He remained so close in the small kitchen she was all fingers and thumbs as she filled a kettle, spooned instant coffee into mugs, fussing with sugar and milk as long as she could until at last he seized her by the shoulders and turned her towards him.

'I don't want coffee,' he said, his face as pale as hers. 'It was just an excuse to stay longer.'

Sophie looked at the smudges of fatigue under his eyes, and felt her anger leach away. 'You look tired, too, Jago.'

'Hard work and lack of sleep.' He drew her a fraction closer. 'I enjoy my job, the publishers are pleased with my book. Life should be good. But it isn't. And you know why, Sophie. So for God's sake tell me you're still of the same mind, because I've changed mine.'

Her eyes lit up with such radiance Jago's snapped shut, and he pulled her against him to take her mouth in a kiss which went on so long they were both panting when he raised his head.

'I just can't go on like this, Sophie,' he said hoarsely, rubbing his cheek against her hair. 'Since Tam's wedding I've had time to think. Life's too short to waste. I agree to your terms. Unconditionally.'

'Weekends of sin?' she whispered against his chest.

'Red-letter days,' he contradicted, and put a finger under her chin so he could look down into her eyes. 'I've a lot more in common with your former lover than I thought.'

'Glen was never my lover,' said Sophie fiercely, then smiled at him with such radiance Jago's eyes darkened in response. 'And you have nothing at all in common with Glen Taylor.'

'Oh, yes, I have. Just like him I want to monopolise every minute of your time you'll give me, Sophie.'

'With you it's different, darling.'

He kissed her hard in response to the endearment. 'You don't know what it does to me to hear you say that.'

'I rather hope,' she whispered, 'that it turns your thoughts to bed. *My* bed. I haven't had a good night's sleep in it since the last time you shared it with me.'

He drew in a deep, unsteady breath, then began kissing her with such mounting purpose, Sophie found it hard to push him away.

'You're staying at the Rose and Crown,' she reminded him, and Jago gave a ragged groan of pure frustration.

'Hell and damnation.' He smiled at her confidently. 'But they've given me a key. I can creep in as late as I like.'

'No, you can't. Go back now.' She smiled a little as his smile vanished. 'Tell them you're going back· to London tonight after all. Then come back here.'

Jago's eyes gleamed. 'Enjoy tormenting me, do you? When I get back I'll exert due retaliation.'

'I'll look forward to that,' she assured him, and with a laugh he seized her in his arms, kissed her hard, then made for the front door.

'You'd better not be asleep,' he warned.

Sophie shook her head. 'I'll count the minutes.'

He gave her a smile which lit up the night, then sprinted down the path.

Sophie closed the door, then went upstairs, hoping she wasn't dreaming. She brushed her hair and thought about changing her flowered cotton pyjamas for something more glamorous, then shook her head at a reflection so bright-eyed and glowing it could have been a different face from the one looming palely in the mirror earlier on. Jago seemed to want her the way she was. And if a night like this now and then, and weekends whenever possible, were all they could have together, the prospect was sheer bliss compared to the wasteland of life without seeing him at all.

Jago took so long Sophie scolded him when she opened the door.

'Where on earth have you been?'

'I thought you might prefer me to park the car discreetly at the Frasers'.' He picked her up and started up the stairs. 'I hope you haven't changed your mind.'

Sophie wreathed her arms round his neck, rubbing her cheek against his. 'Of course I haven't. So take off the James Bond outfit and come to bed.'

CHAPTER ELEVEN

SOPHIE woke in the night in a panic, sure she was dreaming. Then to her overwhelming relief an arm came round her and pulled her close, and a warm, seeking mouth moved over the nape of her neck.

She turned round, the mouth met hers, and she thrust herself against Jago's hard, naked warmth and clutched him close.

'I thought I was dreaming, as usual,' she whispered, when she could.

'Why the hell did we put each other through such misery?' he demanded.

'You did, not me, Jago Langham Smith.'

'But there were extenuating circumstances. With typical male greed I just wanted it all.'

'If things were different nothing would make me happier,' she assured him. 'But I'm here right now in your arms—'

'Where you belong.'

'True. So you can either go on talking, go back to sleep, or...'

'Or?' he prompted, sliding her body beneath his.

'Or,' she said breathlessly, 'you can make love to me.'

Stephen Laing eyed Sophie in remorse when she arrived in her office later than usual next morning.

'You look utterly shattered, Sophie.'

'Sorry I'm late. How's Anna?'

'Had a good night, apparently. She apologises for the hectic time you had yesterday.'

More hectic than the Laings knew, thought Sophie, cheeks hot.

After an early, shared breakfast in bed, Jago had left for London before the rest of Highfield was stirring and, from time to time during the day, Sophie found herself lapsing into daydreams, reliving the night before. In spite of her usual workload, the hours dragged until she could go back to Ivy Lodge for lunch to wait for Jago to ring, and when his call came, on the stroke of one, she curled up on the sofa, her dark-ringed eyes brilliant at the sound of his voice.

'Are you alone, darling?' he asked.

'Yes. Flat out on my sofa.'

He groaned. 'I wish I were flat out with you. Did I mention last night that I'm crazy about you, Miss Marlow?'

'Now and again.'

'And do you reciprocate?'

'Couldn't you tell?'

'Darling, it's going to be a hell of a long time until Friday! Don't drive down. The traffic's always murder. Get a train from Cheltenham and I'll meet you.'

Jago was right. It was an endlessly long week to Sophie, despite their frequent phonecalls. By the time her train drew into Paddington, several minutes late, Sophie had to exert strict control not to shove other passengers out of the way in her haste to reach Jago. He caught her in his arms and kissed her, then picked up her bag and took her off to queue for a taxi.

'We might have a bit of a wait,' he warned, as they joined a lengthy line of people, 'but I didn't fancy getting stuck in traffic in the car.'

Sophie smiled up at him. 'I don't mind waiting.' Which was the simple truth. Now that she was here with Jago, his arm round her, and his eyes smiling down into hers, nothing else in the world mattered.

'I thought we'd stay in tonight,' he said, as they moved gradually along. 'Unless you'd prefer dinner out—'

'No. Let's just catch up on all the time we've wasted.'

Jago's arm tightened. 'Amen to that.'

His new flat occupied the upper half of a solid Victorian house in Islington, with functioning fireplaces in high-ceilinged spacey rooms and an atmosphere of long-established comfort, very different from the smart, modern apartment Sophie had expected.

'You seem surprised,' said Jago, as he showed her round.

She smiled at him. 'I pictured something very different.'

'I bought the place as is, including the furniture,' he said, removing her coat. 'I needed somewhere in a hurry, and one of Charlie's estate agent friends told him the tenant here was in an equal hurry to leave to work abroad. The price was steep, but I was in no mood to dicker, so that was that.'

'I thought you'd have gone for a smart loft apartment with a view of the Thames.'

'Would that be more to your taste?' he said, amused.

Sophie shook her head, looking round in satisfaction. 'No way. I love this place. Add a few touches of your own, Jago, and you'll soon feel as if you'd lived here for ever.'

'But I'll be living here alone,' he reminded her.

'Not all the time.' Sophie gave him a stern look.

'We'll just have to make the most of our weekends together.'

'Starting now,' he agreed, and kissed her nose. 'How about making one of those omelettes you're so good at?'

After supper, when they were curled up together on one of the deep sofas by the log fire Jago had lit, the weeks of hard work and lack of sleep caught up with Sophie, and she fell fast asleep in his arms. She woke hours later, disorientated for a moment, until she realised she was in Jago's bed listening to the sound of his even breathing, and smiled to herself in the darkness as she stretched a little, savouring the pleasure of the discovery.

'What's the matter?' whispered Jago.

'Guilt.'

'Because you're here with me?'

'Because I so rudely fell asleep on you instead of being an entertaining guest.' She turned in his arms to face him, and Jago drew her close.

'You may be an efficient, clever lady in control of her life, Sophie Marlow. But you're also tired and need sleep. In short you're human. Like me.'

'Yes,' she said in a constricted voice. 'Very human. Jago?'

'Yes, my darling.'

'I'm not tired any more.'

He shook with laughter against her. 'Are you making a pass, Miss Marlow?'

Sophie undulated her hips shamelessly. 'Certainly not!'

'Pity.' Jago's voice deepened. 'I hoped you were asking me to make love to you.'

'Do I need to ask?'

'While I live and breathe, never.' He rolled her beneath him, taking his weight on his elbows. 'I promised myself that just holding you, sleeping with you, would be enough,' he said huskily, then let out a groan as she thrust her hips against him.

'Well, it isn't, so stop talking,' she said fiercely, and with a stifled laugh Jago began kissing her mouth and her breasts and every part of her he could reach until at last, driven to desperation, she grasped him with an importunate hand, and with a ragged gasp he lifted her hips and thrust home between thighs which clasped him so convulsively they were soon overtaken by fulfilment so overwhelming it left them breathless and shaken in each other's arms.

The weekend was a revelation to them both. The holiday in Portugal had been magical, but a temporary magic Sophie had known all along would end when they got back to their normal lives. But here, in Jago's comfortable, conventional flat, their time together had a feeling of permanence, fuelled by the knowledge that, short though it might be in the present, in the long-term the pleasure would be regularly renewed.

'This first time,' said Jago, as they breakfasted together the next morning, 'would you mind very much if we didn't go out?'

Sophie looked through the window at rain sheeting down outside. 'Not in the least.'

'Good. My new cleaner did some shopping for me yesterday—'

'So I'm doing the cooking!'

'Just lunch. We'll send out for dinner.' Jago grinned at her, looking a lot different from the haggard man she'd opened her door to only days earlier.

'You may be bored by the time I catch the train tomorrow, Jago.'

'Will *you* be bored?' he demanded.

She shook her head vehemently. 'No. I won't.'

'Neither will I.' He leaned towards her. 'Whenever we've been together lately it's always ended in metaphorical tears—'

'Not so metaphorical on my part,' said Sophie.

Jago took her hand and kissed it. 'You cried?'

'A bit.'

'But not any more!' His eyes softened. 'This time we'll spend the day together, go to bed and wake up together, and tomorrow when we part it won't be the agony of the other times.'

Sophie's fingers tightened on his. 'Longer parting this time, though. Next weekend it's Christmas.'

Jago got up, pulling her with him. 'You're spending it with your family, of course.'

'Of course.' She leaned against him, sliding her arms round his waist. 'How about you?'

'Charlie and I drive off to Norfolk like the good sons we are. But I'll only be there in body,' he added, and smiled down at her crookedly. 'At the risk of sounding mawkish, Sophie Marlow, my heart will be in Wales.'

They spent the weekend together in a rapport which deepened as the time wore on. Determined to put his most significant failure behind her, Sophie was eager to hear about Jago's successes in court, and listened, fascinated, as he painted a word picture of his working life. She listened, rapt, picturing him in the black gown of his calling, the clear-cut, compelling face topped by his barrister's wig.

'My job is interesting enough, but pretty mundane compared with yours,' said Sophie at one point.

'You've worked at Highfield for a fair time,' commented Jago. 'Have you ever thought of moving on somewhere else?'

'Often. But where else would I get a job with a home like Ivy Lodge thrown in?'

'But if you worked somewhere else—here in London, for instance—we'd be able to see more of each other,' he pointed out.

'True.' Sophie eyed him thoughtfully. 'But I'm a cautious soul, Jago. What we have might not last—'

'Of course it will last,' he interrupted, pulling her onto his lap. 'I know that in time there won't be the same desperate need to get you into bed the moment I set eyes on you. But I need you in a way I've never needed anyone before. What we have is what I've been looking for all my adult life.'

She burrowed her head into his shoulder. 'It is for me, too. But you can see my point. If I threw up my job, came here to work in London, what would I do if things don't work out for us after all?'

'I won't change my mind, Sophie,' he said with utter conviction. 'You know damn well I want you for my wife—no—I'm not letting you go, so stop struggling. But,' he went on, 'if not, I'll settle for what we have.'

Sophie subsided against him in full agreement. 'It's a whole lot better than the way things have been these past few weeks.' She looked up at him with narrowed eyes. 'You were utterly horrible to me when I rang you about the letter your brother sent to Glen Taylor.'

'Damn right I was. I thought you'd rung to say you'd changed your mind. To hear you just wanted to pay me money was like a punch in the nose.'

'That was one of the times I cried,' she confessed.

'Did you?' he said softly, and turned her face up to his. 'In that case, my darling, you need some long overdue comfort.'

The only time Jago left the flat was early on Sunday

morning to buy the papers while Sophie made breakfast. They read them together afterwards, prepared lunch together, and it was late that afternoon, when she was reluctantly getting ready to leave for the train, that Sophie came out of the bedroom with a parcel.

'I wasn't sure about this,' she said, handing it to him. 'And if you haven't bought a present for me it doesn't matter in the slightest—'

'Of course I have,' retorted Jago, and hugged her. 'Thank you, darling.'

'You don't even know what it is yet,' she protested, laughing.

'It doesn't matter what it is. You gave it to me, which means the world—' He stopped short, smiling crookedly. 'Just listen to me! None of my colleagues would believe it. There isn't another woman in the world who could affect me like you do, Sophie.'

'There'd better not be! Open it, then.' She eyed him anxiously. 'It's nothing very much, Jago. But it comes with my love.'

He kissed her swiftly, then removed the Christmas paper from a silver photograph frame. From it a sunlit Sophie smiled at him, bright hair loose on bare tanned shoulders, her white cotton sundress blown in the wind.

Jago stared at in silence for so long Sophie began to think she'd made an embarrassing mistake, but at last he enveloped her in a crushing hug. 'Nothing very much, indeed!' He frowned. 'Did I take this?'

'Yes, on the beach. With my camera, the one and only day I remembered to take it out with me. Your photographs reminded me about it, so I had the film developed and bought the frame.' She smiled. 'Do you approve?'

Jago gave her a wry smile. 'If I can't have the subject in the delectable flesh, at least I'll be able to kiss your photograph goodnight instead. Wait there a second,' he added, and went from the room.

He returned with a beribboned package he put in Sophie's lap. 'I would have liked to buy you a ring, but, since you won't allow that, after some searching I found this.'

Sophie unwrapped a long, leather box and took out a necklace created like a gold spider's web dotted with delicate amber drops. She gazed at it in delight, then gave him a blazing, tearwet smile. 'It's exquisite. Thank you, Jago.'

'You can wear it next time you come up,' he said, fastening it round her neck. 'I'll take you out wining, dining, even dancing if you like, as long as it's not a place where they play the rumba!'

Sophie laughed, blinked the tears from her lashes and jumped up to look in the mirror over the mantel. The necklace gleamed against her skin, so delicate, yet such a perfect match with her hair she only wished she could show it to her family.

Jago insisted on getting his car out to drive her to Paddington, but halfway there he astonished her by changing his mind. 'To hell with this. I'll drive you back to Long Ashley and come back in the morning.'

'But Jago—'

'No buts.' He threw her a smile. 'Why waste part of an evening, not to mention a whole night?'

Which was so unanswerable Sophie made no more protests. 'But just this once,' she felt bound to say. 'I don't want you getting too exhausted to—'

'Make love to you?'

'To keep awake in court,' she protested indignantly, then laid a caressing hand on his knee. 'I love you so much, Jago.'

'I love you too, Miss Marlow. But,' he added sternly, 'in the interest of getting there safely, kindly keep your hands to yourself.'

Sophie giggled, suddenly so utterly happy she didn't care about the traffic jamming three lanes of motorway when they joined it. It was enough to be with Jago, who drove, as he did everything else, with such self-confident skill the journey seemed short.

'Aren't you glad I drove you home?' he demanded later, when Sophie unlocked the door of Ivy Lodge.

'Ecstatic!' She grinned impudently as she switched on the hall light. 'Think of the taxi fare you saved me.'

Having expected a lonely return and a restless night spent reliving the dream of the weekend, Sophie's mood was euphoric as she made sandwiches for the supper she wouldn't have bothered with on her own. Jago, in matching mood, was so smugly pleased with himself for his brainwave that Sophie felt bound to kiss him at intervals while she worked, to demonstrate her approval.

'We'll have to go to bed early,' he warned, as he carried a tray into her sitting room.

'All right by me,' she assured him.

Jago grinned. 'Thank you kindly. But it's not just my natural enthusiasm for sharing your bed. I'll have to be up in the small hours to make it back to London in time to get to court, shaved, bewigged and gowned in the persona of J. Langham Smith, Counsel for the Defence.'

'I never heard what the "J" stood for when you defended Ben.' Sophie curled up on the sofa, and offered him the plate of sandwiches. 'What's on tomorrow?'

'Libel case. I'm defending a newspaper which printed some unpalatable facts about a certain public figure.'

'Will you win?'

'Of course. Because the facts in question were the

truth. And,' added Jago, helping himself to another sandwich, 'if the jury believes there is any shred of truth in the defendant's account they are duty-bound to acquit.'

'And you will persuade them to do that?'

'No doubt about it.'

Sophie nodded. 'You're a dangerously persuasive man, Jago Langham Smith.'

'Not all the time. When it comes to you, Sophie Marlow, all the persuasion in the world won't do me any good. You just won't marry me.'

She looked at him steadily. 'But if we did marry our relationship might change, Jago. It might not even work out in the long run. This—this intensity we feel right now would fade. You'd get used to me.'

Jago took her plate and put it with his on the tray, then drew her onto his lap. 'Of course I would. But that's the whole point. I *want* to get used to you, to see you every day, sleep with you every night, to be there if you're ill, or feeling down, as well as happy as a lark like this because we've achieved a few extra hours together.'

'That's such a beautiful thing to say,' she said huskily, and rubbed her cheek against his.

'But it doesn't change your mind.'

Sophie raised her head to look him in the eye. 'If I could marry you I would. Tomorrow. But I can't. I hate having to make rules like this but that's the way it is, Jago. And that's enough soul-searching for one night. So if you've had enough supper let's make a start on this early night you mentioned. Though I warn you,' she added, sliding off his lap, 'I haven't changed my sheets for a day or two.'

'Then what are we waiting for!' said Jago with relish,

and jumped to his feet, arms outstretched. 'Take me, I'm yours.'

During the run-up to Christmas Sophie had less time than usual to miss Jago. Her working days were long, but after the rapturous weekend sleep was a great deal easier to come by. Jago rang her at least once during the day, and always last thing at night when she was in bed. And though she would have expected his verbal love-making to keep her awake, it sent her to sleep happy. During a final call from him, just before she set out to drive home for the holiday, Jago reminded her that they would make up for their Christmas apart by seeing in the New Year at his flat.

'Because we celebrate alone together,' he said firmly. 'After a week apart I've no intention of sharing you with a crowd of carousers, darling.'

Jago had agreed to Sophie's plea for no telephone calls for a day or two, on the understanding that she would call him on the twenty-seventh, after the festivities were over, and Sophie was grateful for his forbearance. Even a call on her mobile phone would mean excusing herself to talk to him in private, followed by a lie about the identity of her caller.

The festival went by with its usual tradition, starting with midnight mass on Christmas Eve. But this year, to Sophie's surprise, Charlotte's parents were coming to lunch on Christmas Day.

'What brought that on?' asked Sophie, as she walked home with her mother from church in the small hours.

'The baby, of course.' Faith shrugged. 'But I'm very pleased for Charlotte. And the Owens are just driving over for lunch, which shouldn't put too much of a strain on the civilities.'

'Do you still feel hostile towards them?'

'No. Because I can see their point. After all, Charlotte is their only child.'

Christmas Day passed in the usual uproar of cooking and present exchanges, and the meal which was surprisingly festive despite the presence of Charlotte's parents. They arrived so obviously anxious to heal the rift that Ben welcomed them into his home with grace, and made it plain he expected his mother and sister to follow suit. Which proved surprisingly easy when everyone was gathered at the festive table in paper hats, laughing over the corny jokes in the Christmas crackers.

On Boxing Day Sophie joined Lucy and Paul at the Red Lion for a lunchtime drink, to find there was more than just Christmas to celebrate after she'd pushed her way through the crowd to find her friends.

'We're engaged,' blurted Lucy.

'Wonderful!' cried Sophie, and hugged them both. 'I'm so pleased for you. Both of you,' she added, and Paul smiled at her in relief.

'Thanks, love. Luce was a tad worried about breaking the news.'

Sophie patted her friend's hand, and admired her ring extravagantly. 'Goose! Why?'

'Nothing to do with Paul and you in the past,' Lucy assured her, and gave her another hug. 'I just wish you could be happy in the same way, that's all.'

'If you mean with Jago, the situation's changed a bit there. I haven't mentioned it over the phone, because it's all a bit new—'

'You mean you're going to marry him after all?' demanded Lucy.

'No, of course not. Things haven't changed that

much.' Sophie smiled like a cat with the cream. 'Jago's agreed to play by my rules, that's all.'

'What does that entail?' asked Paul, grinning.

Lucy fluttered her eyelashes at him. 'Weekends of illicit passion, dearest.' She turned knowing blue eyes on Sophie. 'Not that you had to tell me. I recognised the glow the moment you walked in.'

Heat rose in Sophie's cheeks. 'So don't let me down. When I tell Mother I'm off to London she assumes I mean to you.'

'Won't she find that odd now Luce and I are officially a pair?' asked Paul, frowning.

'Because it's you, no.' Sophie patted his hand. 'Thank goodness Lucy didn't get engaged to someone else.'

'Amen to that,' he said, so fervently his betrothed felt obliged to kiss him by way of appreciation.

'So will you be a bridesmaid again?' asked Faith Marlow, over supper later that night.

'No idea. The wedding's not for ages yet. Lucy won't want Tam's kind of do anyway.'

'Her mother will!'

Sophie smiled. 'In the unlikely event that I plunge into holy matrimony, does that mean you want something like that for me?'

Faith shrugged philosophically. 'I shall do my best to want what you want, darling.'

If only that were possible, thought Sophie wistfully, and changed the subject to Tam, who was spending her first married Christmas with the in-laws.

Next morning Sophie got up early, made breakfast and took a tray in to her mother. 'Stay there for a bit and be lazy,' she ordered. 'You've got your glasses and your new book, so for heaven's sake have a rest. You look tired.'

'How lovely!' Faith Marlow eyed the tempting tray with pleasure. 'Now you've gone to all this trouble I may well wallow here for a bit. What about you?'

'It's rather nice out this morning. I fancy a stroll. See you later.'

Ty Mawr was set in large gardens which made for a pleasant walk in the cold early sunshine, but Sophie had no eyes for her surroundings. When she was far enough from the house she rang Jago's phone, but to her disappointment found he'd switched it off. She made a couple of circuits of the grounds and tried again with the same result. With no real hope of success she rang his flat, and this time reached his answering service, but still no Jago. She left a brief message and rang off unhappily, wondering where he could be. He must have switched off his phone by accident, she assured herself. But with the same result at intervals all afternoon whenever she could snatch some privacy, the feeling of unease persisted all the time she was helping her mother prepare the evening meal Charlotte and Ben were coming round to share.

Sophie kept a determinedly cheerful mask in place when the four of them sat down to enjoy the beef casserole Faith Marlow always cooked at this point over Christmas. And to hide her uneasiness Sophie found a tape of bossa nova rhythms to play in her mother's radio cassette to provide a soothing background as they ate.

'So what are you doing for New Year, Sophie?' asked Ben, filling her glass.

'I'm off to London as usual.' Hopefully.

'Won't you be gooseberry now Lucy's engaged?' said Charlotte, smiling.

'Paul was Sophie's boyfriend first, so they're used to socialising as a threesome,' said Faith cheerfully. 'Odd arrangement, really.'

'But it works,' Sophie assured her. 'Paul was only ever a boyfriend, remember, not the love of my life.'

'High time you found one of those, love,' said Ben, and smiled at his wife. 'I strongly recommend it.'

They were halfway through the meal when the buzzer rang on the door in the little entrance to the flat.

Faith got up in surprise. 'I wonder who that is?' She closed the door behind her and went from the room.

'I hope it's not the vicar,' said Ben, helping himself to seconds from the casserole.

'Why not?' said Sophie. 'Mr Statham's very nice. I met Harry at the wedding, by the way.'

'One of Sophie's old flames,' Ben told his wife. 'The village is littered with them.'

'I wish!' retorted his sister, then looked up with a smile as her mother came in. 'Who was it?'

'A visitor for you, love. In the sitting room. We'll turn the music up louder,' said Faith, and flapped her hand. 'Go on. Shoo!'

Mystified, Sophie crossed the little hall to the sitting room, then slammed the door shut behind her, her eyes wide in furious disbelief when she found Jago Langham Smith waiting for her, tense, like a man expecting a blow.

CHAPTER TWELVE

'WHAT exactly are you doing here?' Sophie asked, deadly quiet, her anger overriding the instinctive urge to throw herself into his arms.

'What I should have insisted on doing ever since we got back from Portugal,' he returned, equally quiet.

'Even though you knew it was the last thing in the world I wanted?'

Jago moved towards her, arms outstretched, but dropped them abruptly at her gesture of fierce repudiation. 'I've had a lot of time to think over Christmas,' he said, his eyes boring into hers. 'I'm no gambler, but I decided it was time to chance the biggest gamble of my life. I love you more than I thought I would ever love anyone, Sophie. And in three years I'll be forty. Until I met you I never felt the lack of a wife or children. But now I do. I want to share *all* my life with you, not just the few hours together you're prepared to give me.' He shrugged. 'So instead of driving to London today as planned I came on here, to seek out your family and ask for their—'

'Forgiveness?' she cut in stonily.

His eyes narrowed. 'Actually, no. I came to ask their blessing. To tell them I love you. That I have a perfectly natural urge to make you legally mine. The same thing any normal, red-blooded man wants when he finds his mate.'

'Regardless of the feelings of said "mate",' said Sophie, her voice shaking with anger. 'I can't believe

you've done this, Jago. You know how much my family
means to me—'

'None better since you put them before me at every
turn,' he retorted.

'And that's the problem, of course.' She glared at him.
'You need to come first in the pecking order every time!'

'That's not true.' Jago took up a stance she could tell
was one he automatically assumed to argue his cases in
court. 'I just want recognition of my status in your life.
Husband, partner—whatever you want, Sophie, as long
as it's exclusive and your family knows about it. I'm
willing to risk the fact that they might never accept me
as part of their circle.' His face set. 'But I just can't go
on with this deception.'

Sophie's chin lifted. 'Then there's no more to be said.
Because I want no part of a relationship where you call
all the shots. You knew very well how I felt about this,
yet you still took it on yourself to make a unilateral
decision which concerned *my* family. I can't forgive
that.'

'Sophie—' Jago took a step towards her, then halted
as she backed away, his eyes hard. 'I've obviously made
the biggest mistake of my life.'

'If you mean your gamble, yes. It didn't come off.
And not only that,' she added with sudden passion,
'you've forced me to tell the others I've been seeing you
in secret anyway. How could you *do* this to me?'

His eyes burned with sudden anger. 'You know damn
well I did it for us, Sophie. For our future together.'

'Then you needn't have troubled. Because due to your
disregard for my feelings on the subject, we don't have
a future any more. Of any kind. I never want to see you
again. Ever.' Trembling with temper, resentment, and
something she refused to acknowledge as sheer physical

longing for him, she flung away to the door, but it opened before she could reach it, and Faith came in, followed by Ben and Charlotte.

Sophie stood rooted to the spot in horror, but to her amazement Ben came forward, hand outstretched, smiling with a warmth which astonished her.

'Hello there! This is unexpected,' he said, as Jago shook his hand. 'Mother tells me you know my little sister rather better than she's been letting on.'

'I'm afraid so,' said Jago, avoiding Sophie's eyes. 'I thought it was time to come out of hiding and plead my cause.'

Ben's steady brown eyes met equally steady grey for a moment, then he nodded and drew Charlotte forward. 'This is my wife. Charlotte, meet Jago Langham Smith.'

Jago shook her hand, smiling crookedly. 'Alias the villain of the piece where Sophie's concerned, Mrs Pritchard.'

'I know all about that.' Charlotte smiled at him serenely. 'Though to be fair you had no chance with a defendant who insisted on pleading guilty.'

'Because I was,' said Ben matter-of-factly. 'I stole the money—'

'Borrowed it,' contradicted his mother.

'In the eyes of the law I stole it, Ma. But I count myself fortunate in having a barrister who did the very best he could for me with the judge—won me the shortest sentence possible.' He gave her a swift hug, then turned to Jago. 'Have you eaten? Sophie was only halfway through her dinner when you arrived.'

'Mr Langham Smith isn't staying,' said Sophie flatly.

'Nonsense!' Faith frowned at her in disapproval. 'He's driven a long way, so he must at least stay for a meal before he goes on his way. Are you returning to London tonight, Mr—?'

'Jago,' he said swiftly. 'I'm putting up at the Red Lion.'

'Then I shall reheat the remains of our casserole, and you shall eat it while the rest of us get to grips with pudding and cheese,' said Faith firmly, ignoring the killing look her daughter threw at her.

And, seethe as much as she might, Sophie was powerless to prevent Jago Langham Smith from receiving the same treatment all her mother's guests enjoyed. But she sat mute and resentful at table, refusing to join in the conversation, and turned down all offers of food. While Jago, to her fury, did full justice to the reheated beef casserole, and to the cheese which followed it.

And afterwards, to fill her cup to the brim, Sophie was informed that she could have the pleasure of clearing away, because Jago had requested a few minutes with her mother and brother.

'I'll help,' said Charlotte promptly, but Faith shook her head.

'No dear. Sophie can manage. This concerns you, too.'

Surely it concerns me even more? thought Sophie, incensed. She slammed the door shut, tuned the radio to the loudest selection of rock music she could find and marched back and forth to the kitchen with leftover food and dirty plates. She stacked the dishwasher with a force which threatened her mother's dinner service, cleared the cloth from the dining room table, replaced the silver pheasants which normally sat on it, then proceeded to clean the kitchen to within an inch of its life to prevent herself from storming into the other room.

Not, she assured herself, that it mattered a damn what

Jago was saying or asking, or what response he was getting. Because even if her family welcomed him as her prospective bridegroom with open arms she had no intention of marrying a man who steamrollered over every rule she'd laid down for their relationship.

When the kitchen was immaculate Sophie went to her room and took steps to ensure that her own person was equally immaculate. Hair gleaming on the shoulders of a new pink sweater it blended with surprisingly well, make-up renewed to the last flick of mascara, Sophie marched out into the hall to find her mother waiting to waylay her.

'You, my girl,' said Faith with unexpected anger, 'are behaving like a spoilt child. Come into the kitchen. I want a word.'

The wind taken completely out of her sails, Sophie complied as though she were six instead of twenty years older than that.

'Jago shouldn't have come,' she said, and winced as she heard the petulance in her own voice. 'He had no right to give you a shock like that.'

'The only shock I've had tonight came from your bad manners,' retorted Faith.

'I'm sorry.' Sophie took in a deep breath. 'I apologise. Not just for my manners, but for not telling you about Jago before.'

'My dear child, I've known about him ever since Tam's wedding!'

Sophie stared. 'How?'

'Falling in love must have addled your wits, girl.' Faith shook her head. 'We live in a village where everyone knows you, Sophie. Olwen Probert wasn't the only one who told me you walked from the church with Jasper Hayford's oldest friend. And sat with him at the reception, where, by all accounts, it was obvious that he was no stranger to you. Not to mention the fact that you were seen leaving the dance together.'

'Why didn't you tell me?' demanded Sophie angrily.

'I was waiting for you to tell *me*. It didn't take much grey matter to realise that if his identity was a deadly secret Jasper's old friend had to be the one he asked to defend Ben.'

Sophie slumped down on a kitchen chair. 'You'd better hear the whole story, then.'

'I don't need to. Jago's just told us everything. Including the holiday in Portugal you were supposed to have spent with Lucy.' Faith sat down opposite, her dark eyes softening. 'He also told us that at first you wouldn't have anything to do with him. Because of Ben.'

'And because of you, too.' Sophie eyed her mother wearily. 'You blamed Jago bitterly at one time, remember. I assumed Ben blamed him too.'

'He never has. As far as Ben's concerned Jago did his very best for him, pleaded extenuating circumstances, a first offence, stressed the intention to repay, and asked for the lightest sentence possible. I was the one who blamed Jago.' Faith sighed. 'I needed a scapegoat. Someone to assuage my guilt. Because Ben did what he did for me. Mr Langham Smith, as I always thought of him, did the very best he could for Ben. It's been a very long time since I blamed him for my son's prison sentence.'

So it had all been for nothing. Sophie raked a hand through her hair in despair. 'What did Jago say to you?' she asked at last.

'He told me he'd come to ask for our blessing, or, if we couldn't stretch to that, at least to consider the idea of him as your husband.'

'And what did you say?'

'Ben leapt in with complete approval before I could say a word. Sort of handed you over on a platter.' Faith's eyes twinkled.

'Did he now?' Sophie's eyes kindled. 'And how about you, Mother?'

'With rather more restraint I made it clear my sentiments were much the same. I like him, Sophie. It took guts for Jago to come and confront us here like this. If I were you I'd be very, very flattered.'

'Well, I'm not.'

'Something you made very plain.' Faith smiled ruefully. 'So plain, in fact, that after stating his case Jago told us that he was very grateful for our approval, but unfortunately it was academic. According to Jago you never want to see him again. Which is a case of cutting off your nose to spite your face if ever I heard one!'

'He had no right to come marching in here against my wishes, Mother,' said Sophie stormily.

'So you indulged in the best tantrum I've witnessed since you were four years old,' said Faith, shaking her head. 'You're crazy about him, aren't you?'

'Not any more.' Sophie got up. 'I'd better go to Ben and Charlotte's rescue and speed Jago Langham Smith on his way.'

'No need.' Faith got up and put her arm round her daughter. 'That's what I came in to say. After stating his case, and receiving our no longer necessary approval, Jago thanked us very gracefully, shook hands all round, and left.'

'*What?*' Sophie stared at her mother in horror. 'You let him go?'

'Darling, I know Jago less intimately than you, it's true, but something tells me his isn't the type you *let* do anything. When you said you never wanted to see him again he obviously thought you meant it. Which,' added Faith tartly, 'serves you right, my girl. Perhaps if you drive to the Red Lion right away you might convince him you didn't mean it. Though after the performance you put on tonight I wouldn't blame him if his offer was no longer open.'

But Sophie wasn't listening. She flew into her room for her car keys and a jacket, hurtled down the stairs to the car park, then drove as fast as she dared to the village. Inside the Red Lion she went straight to the bar to buttonhole her old school friend, Ian Cook, who was helping his father out, as he always did during a visit home. He welcomed her with enthusiasm, told her she looked gorgeous, and asked what she wanted to drink.

'Nothing, thanks, Ian. Just tell me the room number of one of your guests. Name of Langham Smith.'

'Sorry, love, he left a short while ago. Didn't stay the night after all.'

Sophie felt as if every last drop of blood was draining from her veins. 'Oh, well, never mind,' she managed. 'See you, Ian.'

She drove back to Ty Mawr very slowly, facing the fact that Jago had taken her dismissal at face value. When she let herself in to the flat Ben and Charlotte were talking earnestly with Faith. All three of them looked up hopefully when she went in, but after one look at her face Charlotte got up and held her close.

'He's gone,' said Sophie brokenly.

During the long, sleepless night which followed Sophie came to a decision. Since meeting Jago Langham Smith her life had see-sawed between euphoric happiness and the blackest of misery. She just couldn't go on like this.

She wanted her life back the way it was before, well-ordered, lived by her own rules. And now Jago would no longer be part of it that could be achieved. Eventually. And if it sounded deadly dull, so be it. Dull was good. Infinitely preferable to agony. Which was all the more agonising because it was self-inflicted. In her fury at having her precious rules broken she'd thrown away something so precious she would never find anything remotely like it again.

Next day Faith Marlow was infinitely tactful in her dealings with her crushed, miserable daughter. She gave Sophie breakfast in bed, told her to stay there as long as she liked, and announced she was having lunch with Olwen Probert in Usk. She gave Sophie a list of available things she could have for her own lunch, then took herself off for the day, promising to be back by late afternoon.

'Thank you, Mother,' said Sophie, and managed a smile. 'By the time you get back I might be better company.'

'You won't be here.'

'What do you mean?'

'You and Lucy are having tea with Tam, remember. To admire the love-nest. Had you forgotten?'

Sophie groaned. 'One way and another it slipped my mind.'

'I'm sure it did, darling,' said Faith, and bent to kiss her. 'Do you good, though. You've got hours to get in the mood.'

Sophie got up after her mother left, had a bath, spent a long time on her hair and eventually, wearing black sweater and jeans to match her mood, considered the idea of lunch. She rejected it in favour of a walk in the grounds of Ty Mawr, and found Lucy waiting for her when she got back to the house.

'Paul went back this morning, my mother's whooping it up with yours, so I thought I'd come round and park myself on you.'

'I'm not much company at the moment,' warned Sophie.

'I know. Your mother said I must tread carefully, because you've sent Jago packing. Again. You're nuts,' added Lucy candidly. 'Whatever happened to sensible Sophie?'

'Jago Langham Smith happened. But this time it's really over. And I don't want to talk about it, Luce.'

Lucy took her at her word, and talked of everything under the sun other than her own wedding plans. And Jago Langham Smith. By the time they were ready to leave for Ilex Cottage Sophie was feeling a little better. Not happy. But better.

'Let's walk,' said Lucy. 'I don't get enough exercise in London.'

'No one would know it,' Sophie assured her, eyeing her friend's long, lean shape. 'I eat one chocolate bar and it shows.'

'Then you haven't eaten one lately,' said Lucy bluntly. 'Christmas pudding or not, you've lost weight since I saw you last.'

Tam's new home was a comfortable, welcoming place, full of flowers and cushions, and with a roaring log fire in the inglenook fireplace in what she called the parlour. She hugged her friends, drew their attention to the ranks of wedding photographs in silver frames on every surface, and plied them with crumpets she toasted on an antique fork the Judge had found in the recesses of Hayford House.

'Every time he comes over he brings me something,' she said happily, and beamed at them. 'Especially now I'm pregnant.'

'Already?' said Lucy, astonished.

'I've been married for two and a half months, Luce.' Tam gurgled. 'It doesn't take long to get pregnant!'

Sophie felt a sharp stab of envy as she jumped up to hug Tam. 'No doubt David's over the moon?'

Tam nodded complacently. 'Daddy is too. He's convinced my baby will be a girl.'

The three of them sat talking together over endless cups of tea, and Sophie took over the toasting fork after discovering that hot buttered crumpet wasn't a bad idea after several hours without food.

Later on Tam put a guard in front of the fire and announced that they were all expected back at Hayford House for drinks. 'Daddy's determined to ply you girls with liquor.'

'Why not?' said Sophie recklessly. 'A small libation wouldn't come amiss.'

'Or even a big one,' said Lucy with relish, and held Sophie's suede jacket for her.

'That's gorgeous,' said Tam in admiration. 'The exact colour of your hair. Christmas present?'

'From all three of my loved ones because it was so expensive,' said Sophie, smoothing a lapel.

They walked across the green through the darkness of the crisp December evening, to see the Judge standing in the open doorway of Hayford House to welcome them. He gave all three girls a hug and a kiss, then ushered them through the hall and into the garden room at the back of the house.

'Drinks in here,' he announced. 'Look sharp, lads, I've brought some ladies to join you.'

Jasper rushed forward for more hugs and kisses, but his companion remained where he was, still and silent, near the door to the garden.

Sophie emerged from Jasper's embrace and, ignoring Lucy's tense face, smiled with hard-won composure at Jago. 'Hello. I thought you'd gone back to London.'

'I was at the pub when Jago came in last night,' said Jasper. 'I could hardly let him put up there with empty bedrooms to spare in this place.'

'Quite right, son,' said the Judge, and sat down by the table with the drinks tray. 'Now then, my dears, how about some champagne?'

Jago moved forward to greet Tam and Lucy, but kept well away from Sophie other than to acknowledge her greeting with an unsmiling nod.

Hoping it would dull the pain this inflicted, Sophie accepted the champagne Jasper offered. And after drinking some of it found she was able to join in the conversation with reasonable animation, and second the toasts the Judge made to his future grandchild.

'You're very silent, Smithy, my boy,' said the judge. 'Still recovering from that hangover?'

'Afraid so, sir,' said Jago, smiling faintly.

Jasper pulled a face. 'We managed to down quite a tot or two last night. More than was wise, I found this morning. My head's only just beginning to recover.'

'One good thing,' said the Judge comfortably. 'It means we've managed to persuade our guest to stay another night. Can't drive back to London until his alcohol level subsides.'

'You should stick to orange juice, like me,' said Tam, and began passing round dishes of nuts. 'Do have some of these or I'll eat the lot. I can't stop nibbling these days.'

The conversation became general, and at any other time Sophie would have enjoyed sparring with the Judge and flirting with Jasper, as she'd done so often in the past. But with Jago watching in saturnine detachment the pastime lost its appeal.

'It's been lovely, but I really must go,' she said at last, and got up. 'Mother must be back by now.'

Tam clapped a hand to her mouth. 'Oh, sorry. I should have told you. Sophie, your mother rang to leave a message before you arrived, said she'd missed you at home. She's going on to Ben's after the trip to Usk, and may be late. Sorry I forgot.' She made a face. 'Blame it on the hormones.'

'No need for you to rush away then, Sophie my dear,' said the Judge. 'Sit down and have another drink.'

'And after that you and Lucy come home and have supper with me,' said Tam. 'David won't be home until late tonight.'

'Sorry,' said Sophie in desperation. 'I really must get on with packing and so on. I'll take a raincheck.'

'But you can come, Luce,' said Tam, disappointed.

'Of course I will,' said Lucy promptly. 'I'm sure one of these gentlemen will walk Sophie home.'

Jasper opened his mouth to offer his services, then closed it again at a look from Lucy.

There was an awkward little silence for a moment, then Jago picked up Sophie's jacket.

'A stroll is just what I need to clear my head,' he said, as he held it for her.

Oh, well, thought Sophie, as she slid her arms into the sleeves. Who wants a dull life anyway?

After a noisy leavetaking, during which Sophie was hugged by her friends and kissed very soundly by the Hayford men, she set off with Jago in silence which deepened as they left the village for the unlit road beyond. It was very much colder than earlier on, and she was glad of the long black wool scarf around her neck when an icy little wind came whistling through the hedges. Jago was wearing an old leather windbreaker with a roll-necked sweater and heavy moleskins, and seemed impervious to the cold. Also untroubled by the silence which rapidly grew unbearable to Sophie. At last she could stand it no longer.

'I'm sorry,' she blurted.

'What for exactly?' enquired Jago.

She breathed in deeply. 'That I behaved like a spoilt child last night. My mother was appalled by my bad manners.'

'So you're apologising for your manners,' he observed without inflection.

This wasn't going the way Sophie intended. 'Not only that,' she said in desperation. 'I was so thrown by having you turn up like that I said things I—I regretted afterwards.'

'You said you never wanted to see me again,' he reminded her.

'At the time I meant it.'

'I could tell.'

Silence fell again for a while.

Sophie tried again. 'I didn't expect you to leave so suddenly.'

'I'd said everything I came to say. To your brother and your mother. And,' added Jago very deliberately, 'from my point of view, Sophie, you said more than enough. So I took myself off.'

'I went after you. To the Red Lion. But Ian Cook said you'd gone.'

'Who's Ian Cook?'

'Son of the landlord. Old school friend.'

'One of the many.'

Sophie marshalled her forces. This was hard work. But Jago needn't have offered to walk her home, she thought, brightening. 'I thought you'd gone to London.'

'It was certainly my intention,' he admitted. 'But I ran into Jasper in the pub, and he insisted on taking me home to stay the night. After the welcome *you* dished out Jasper's was just what I needed. Good company and quantities of malt whisky were a great comfort after my treatment at your fair hands.'

She winced. 'I've said I'm sorry.'

'So you have.'

By this time they'd reached the brightly lit drive of Ty Mawr. Sophie looked up at the face of the man beside her, but it gave no clue to his feelings. Jago was playing his cards close to his chest.

'Would you like to come in?' she asked awkwardly.

He eyed her for a moment, as though weighing up his answer, then shrugged. 'Very well. Just for a moment.'

'Don't put yourself out,' snapped Sophie, and turned on her heel, but Jago caught her by the elbow before she got to the entrance.

'I never realised you had such a temper,' he observed, his fingers like a vice.

Sophie tried to free herself, but with a grip of iron Jago marched her into the lift and pressed the ascent button. And as soon as the doors closed on them he pulled her into his arms, smothered her protests with his mouth, and went on kissing her until the lift opened on the top landing and they surfaced to find a smartly dressed woman eyeing them in fascination.

Sophie emerged, crimson, from Jago's embrace, and managed a smile. 'Good evening, Miss Howells. How are you?'

'Very well indeed,' said Faith Marlow's neighbour, and smiled at Jago. 'I think we passed in the hall last night.'

'Jago Langham Smith,' he said, returning the smile, and held out his hand. 'I'm a friend of Sophie's.'

'I rather gathered that,' she said, laughing, and went into the lift.

Without looking at Jago, Sophie hurried along the hall to her mother's door, but her hand was so unsteady she had trouble with the key. Jago took it from her, unlocked the door, and followed her inside.

Sophie switched on a couple of lamps. And only then turned to face the relentless grey eyes fixed on her face. 'I've got something to say.'

Jago folded his arms. 'Say it then.'

'It's a quotation.'

He raised a sardonic eyebrow. 'From your favourite poet?'

'No. From you.' Sophie cleared her throat. '"For God's sake",' she quoted very deliberately, '"tell me you're still of the same mind. Because I've changed mine."'

Jago stood very still. 'Clarify,' he commanded.

In for a penny, in for a pound, decided Sophie. 'Will you marry me, Jago? Please?'

He closed the space between them in one stride,

caught the ends of her scarf and unwound it, then took her in his arms, his eyes blazing with triumph mingled with relief. 'Since you ask so nicely, how can I refuse?' he teased, and kissed her very gently, a caress utterly different from the punitive embrace in the lift. He raised his head to smiled down into her eyes. 'I thought you never wanted to see me again. Ever.'

'I changed my mind,' she said gruffly.

'When did you do that?'

'About two minutes after I said it.' She gazed at him in remorse. 'I'm sorry I was such a shrew, Jago. I lost my temper. I really don't do that very often these days. And in future I'll make it a rule—'

'Sophie,' interrupted Jago. 'Before we go any further I insist on making a rule of my own.'

'Oh, yes?' She leaned back against his encircling arms, eyeing him warily. 'What is it?'

'That there'll be no more rules of any kind from now on.' He smiled triumphantly. 'That way neither of us will break any.'

'Done!' She laughed and hugged him close, and Jago picked her up and sat down with her on the sofa.

'Do you think your mother would mind,' he muttered, in between kisses, 'if I steal you off to London tomorrow?'

'I hope not, because I'm coming anyway,' she assured him. 'Not that she will mind. Mother strongly approves of, I quote, your guts in coming here last night.'

'It took some doing,' he admitted. 'But the prize was worth it. So come on, time we went round to Ben's place to give your family the glad news.' Jago tipped her face up to his. 'If only you'd let me meet them sooner you and I could have avoided a great deal of misery, Sophie Marlow.'

'I realise that now.' She slid off his lap and stood looking down at him. 'You'll have to tell me the best way to make it up to you.'

Jago jumped up and caught her to him. 'As I've said before, my darling—just improvise.'

EPILOGUE

MOONLIGHT poured over the garden of the Quinta Viana, forming patterns on the floor of the bedroom Jago insisted on calling the bridal chamber.

'But we've slept here before,' Sophie had protested, laughing when he carried her over the threshold earlier.

'It felt like a bridal chamber then, too,' he'd assured her.

Now it was well into the night, and the two occupants of the tester bed lay quiet, but wide awake, needing to savour every moment of their wedding night.

'We can sleep any other night,' said Jago, smoothing a hand over his wife's hair.

'True. Besides, I don't feel sleepy. Though I should,' added Sophie, wriggling closer.

'Because we've already made love? And if you keep on doing that it's more than probable we will again,' he warned.

'It's standard procedure for wedding nights,' his bride informed him.

'Standard is entirely the wrong word for the feelings you arouse in me, Mrs Langham Smith.'

'Oh, how lovely!'

'The feelings?'

'Those too. But it was the Mrs Langham Smith bit I liked even more.'

'I like it, too. Not least because it was such damned hard work getting you to agree to it.'

'I wanted to marry you right from the first.' Sophie

clasped his hand tightly. 'You were so muffled up against the rain I could only see your eyes that first night when you came knocking on my door. But I had a strong feeling of recognition, as though I'd seen you before.'

Jago turned her to face him. 'You had, unfortunately.'

'Yes. But long before the trial.' Sophie sat up, reached out to switch on a lamp, then slid back down into his arms. 'I've got a story to tell. You and I first came into contact years before that, Mr Langham Smith.'

Jago frowned, intrigued. 'Go on then, Scheherazade.'

'I only discovered it myself yesterday, after the wedding. Tam told me.'

'Where does Tam come into this?'

'A long time ago I was staying with her, on a very cold winter night, and to get warm she insisted we both creep into her brother's bed.' Sophie grinned at the look dawning in Jago's eyes. 'She didn't know Jasper had given his bed up to his friend. Tam's nanny found us missing next morning, ran us to earth, horrified, and managed to whisk us out of bed without waking you up.'

Jago stared at her incredulously. 'I can't believe this. I've actually married the woman who gave me the worst night of my entire life!'

'Want a divorce?'

'No.' His eyes gleamed. 'Though it may take several years of very different nights to make it up to me.'

'I think I can manage that.' Sophie promised happily. 'The Judge was furious with us, by the way.'

Jago blenched. 'He *knew*?'

'Oh, yes. The nanny marched us into him straight away and made Tam confess.'

Jago shuddered. 'He never said a word.'

'He said enough to Tam—who never did it again.'

Sophie smiled at him. 'I had only a fleeting glimpse of you as we were bundled out. But it must have stayed in my subconscious, because I had this strong feeling of *déjà vu* that night in the rain, even before I discovered who you were. And I read somewhere that one must have met, or seen, someone before to get the feeling so vividly.'

'Vivid's the word,' he said with feeling. 'Can you imagine my reaction when I woke up in the night to find myself in bed with two little girls? And in the house of the far from lenient Judge Hayford, at that!'

Sophie dissolved into laughter, and hugged him close. 'But now,' she said, against his chest, 'they're both big girls—and one of them's legally yours.'

'Which works both ways, my darling bride.' Jago turned her face up to his and kissed her. 'I'm legally yours, too.'

'You bet your life you are,' she informed him, and slid a hand down his spine. 'But in case you need reminding...'

Modern Romance™
...seduction and
passion guaranteed

Tender Romance™
...love affairs tha
last a lifetime

Sensual Romance™
...sassy, sexy and
seductive

Blaze
...sultry days and
steamy nights

Medical Romance™
...medical drama on
the pulse

Historical Romance™
...rich, vivid and
passionate

29 new titles every month.

*With all kinds of Romance for
every kind of mood...*

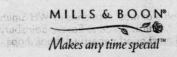

MILLS & BOON®

Makes any time special™

MAT4

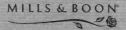

FREE
2 BOOKS
AND A SURPRISE GIFT!

We would like to take this opportunity to thank you for reading this Mills & Boon® book by offering you the chance to take TWO more specially selected titles from the Modern Romance™ series absolutely FREE! We're also making this offer to introduce you to the benefits of the Reader Service™ —

- ★ FREE home delivery
- ★ FREE monthly Newsletter
- ★ FREE gifts and competitions
- ★ Exclusive Reader Service discount
- ★ Books available before they're in the shops

Accepting these FREE books and gift places you under no obligation to buy; you may cancel at any time, even after receiving your free shipment. Simply complete your details below and return the entire page to the address below. *You don't even need a stamp!*

YES! Please send me 2 free Modern Romance™ books and a surprise gift. I understand that unless you hear from me, I will receive 4 superb new titles every month for just £2.49 each, postage and packing free. I am under no obligation to purchase any books and may cancel my subscription at any time. The free books and gift will be mine to keep in any case.

P1ZEC

Ms/Mrs/Miss/Mr ....Initials ....
BLOCK CAPITALS PLEASE

Surname ....

Address ....

....

....Postcode ....

Send this whole page to:
UK: FREEPOST CN81, Croydon, CR9 3WZ
EIRE: PO Box 4546, Kilcock, County Kildare (stamp required)